Drowned

THERESE BOHMAN

*Translated from the Swedish
by Marlaine Delargy*

OTHER PRESS   NEW YORK

Poetry excerpts on pages 27 and 146 from "Ophelia" by Arthur Rimbaud, translation derived from the English translation by Oliver Bernard in *Collected Poems* (New York: Penguin Classics, 1997). Copyright
© Oliver Bernard, 1962, 1997. Poetry excerpt on page 61 from "Song"
[When I Am Dead, My Dearest] by Christina Rossetti, first published
in 1862. Poetry excerpts on pages 105 and 200–201 from "Dolores" by
Algernon Charles Swinburne, first published in 1866.

Production Editor: Yvonne E. Cárdenas
Text Designer: Cassandra J. Pappas
This book was set in 11 pt Elektra by Alpha Design & Composition
of Pittsfield, NH.

10 9 8 7 6 5 4 3 2 1

Library of Congress Cataloging-in-Publication Data

Bohman, Therese, 1978–
  [Den drunknade. English]
  Drowned / by Therese Bohman ; translated by Marlaine Delargy.
     p. cm.
  ISBN 978-1-59051-524-2 (trade pbk. : acid-free paper) — ISBN 978-
1-59051-525-9 (e-book)
  1. Sisters—Fiction. 2. Family secrets—Fiction. 3. Triangles
(Interpersonal relations)—Fiction. 4. Sweden—Fiction.
I. Delargy, Marlaine. II. Title.
  PT9877.12.O48D7813 2012
  839.73'8—dc23

                                                        2011049352

The self-same force which drives up myriad
    shoots through clinging mud,
spins threads through tender stems and in a
    flower's bud,
brews sumptuous, scented oils, weaves petals'
    gossamer glow—
lives in our very being, deep, deep down below.

                    —OLA HANSSON, *Notturno*

Part One

The train is exactly on time as it pulls into the platform. My whole body feels listless as I stand up and get my bag down from the luggage rack above the window. There's something wrong with my seat, with the mechanism that's supposed to stop the back-rest when you've reclined it into the position you want. I've been pushed backwards every time the train has accelerated, and several times during the journey I have woken up and discovered that I am practically lying down. I don't like reclining seats too far back, the feeling of them disappearing behind me always makes me think of a visit to the dentist.

I haul my suitcase off the rack at the end of the carriage as the train stops and the doors glide open.

The heat hits me like a wall, the air is oppressive, not much cooler than the air inside the train, and the sunlight is so bright that it hurts my eyes, I have to blink several times. I feel like I've just woken up, my ears are still buzzing from hurtling through a tunnel, I feel as if I've been on a plane rather than a train. I don't like traveling, even if trains are better than planes, less brutal. You have time to get used to the idea that you're on the way to a different place.

I squint my eyes and see Stella a short distance away down the platform, she is on time too, of course. When she sees me she smiles with her whole face, waves, and hurries toward me. My hands are sticky from the heat and the sweets I ate on the train, but of course she doesn't shake my hand, she puts her arms around me and pulls me close and I hug her back. The scent of her is familiar, she smells the same as always. Cool.

"How was your journey?" she says. She sounds happy.

"Fine. It just took a long time, that's all."

She nods, points toward the small newsstand on the station concourse.

"The car is just around the corner. Do you need any help with your luggage?"

"No, it's okay."

She already has her own bag to carry, a brown leather purse that looks expensive. Her entire look is expensive; she's wearing a beige skirt and a chalk-white blouse, she looks clean and crisp, as if her clothes have been hung out to dry in the wind coming off the sea, starched by the salt in the air so they didn't even need ironing. Small pearl studs gleam in her ears. I feel dusty, and the sweets have left a stale taste in my mouth. I would like to brush my teeth.

"I told Gabriel to start on dinner," she says as we walk toward the car, the wheels of my suitcase trundling over the cracks in the paving stones outside the station, a few gulls circling high above. "Are you hungry?"

I actually feel slightly nauseous, but it wouldn't be very polite to say so. Instead I nod and she smiles at me, jangling the car keys in her hand.

We drive along past fields of corn. The sun is still beating down mercilessly in spite of the fact that it is nearly evening, the sky is an almost unreal shade of blue, like a vast dome over the open landscape. Stella has put on a pair of dark oversized sunglasses. Mine are in my suitcase, so I have to carry on squinting. She presses a button on the car's sound system, it's New Order—*In the end you will submit, it's got to hurt a little bit.* Stella drums her index fingers on the steering wheel, glances at me and smiles, I smile back. We have time to listen to several more tracks before we arrive. Stella turns off the main road onto a smaller one, then onto a gravel road pitted with pot-holes. Dust swirls up behind us and pebbles clatter against the undercarriage of the car, it sounds like a hailstorm. There are still fields of crops on either side, weeds growing in the ditches, thistles gray with dust.

The gravel road ends at a small parking space in front of a yellow wooden house. It's a beautiful place, with a glassed-in balcony above the large veranda. The garden is full of mature fruit trees, farther away I can see flower beds and rows of vegetables. A black cat is lying on the steps but is woken by the sound of the car engine and slowly ambles away. Stella jumps energetically out of the car, I still feel drowsy.

"Come on, I'll show you around!"

"I just need to go to the bathroom."

She looks annoyed for a moment, then seems to realize that this is a perfectly reasonable request. She opens the trunk and lifts out my case, which lands on the gravel with a heavy thud. She smiles at me.

"Have you brought the entire contents of the library with you?"

I'm smiling too.

"I'll give you a hand."

Together we carry the bags across the parking area and along a narrow path with sparsely laid-out paving stones, up the steps to the front door and in through a bamboo curtain, the rattling sound makes me think of a xylophone. Inside, the house is warm and smells of wood, dry and slightly stuffy in a way that is not unpleasant but feels quite homely, like a summer cottage. The hallway is dark but the kitchen is large and light, and the man who is Gabriel is standing by the sink rinsing bright-green sugar snap peas in an old colander. He is tall and dark.

"Gabriel, this is Marina."

His handshake is firm and his hands are big. His smile is also big as he says it's good to meet me at last, he stares at me for a moment, gazing into my eyes until I have to look away. Then they start talking about the food, he says he couldn't get hold of what he wanted for the salad, the store is useless.

Stella looks at me and nods toward the door.

"There's a bathroom in the hall."

I take my purse with me and when I look in the mirror above the washbasin I think I should have tidied myself up before I got off the train. I look pale, and my forehead is shiny. My hair is flat and looks dry and brittle, perhaps because of the air-conditioning on the train. I have a pee, then quickly touch up my makeup before running my hands through my hair to try to get some volume into it.

Gabriel is still busy with the salad when I get back to the kitchen, he is slicing radishes very thinly.

"Your sister's gone to get changed," he says.

I nod. "Can I do anything?"

"No, it's almost ready. Besides which, this is your welcome dinner . . . so all you have to do is feel welcome."

He smiles.

"Can I get you anything? Something to drink?"

Suddenly I realize I'm thirsty. I should have cleaned my teeth, my mouth still feels sweet and sticky.

"That would be lovely."

"A glass of wine?"

"I'd prefer water, I think I'm getting a headache."

Gabriel looks concerned.

"Do you often get headaches?"

"No . . . not really."

"Stella does," he says. "I wondered if it was something that runs in the family."

"I don't think so."

He opens one of the kitchen cupboards and rummages around until he finds a box of painkillers, which he holds up to show me.

"Would you like one of these?"

I nod. "Yes please."

He runs me a glass of water and passes me the box. The water is so cold it's almost difficult to hold the glass. I push one tablet through the silver foil. It makes a muted rustling sound, which I like, I've liked it ever since I was a little girl. The coldness of the water produces a stabbing sensation in my head, a moment of unpleasantness before I feel as if my mind is sharpening. I empty the glass in long gulps, the water tastes different out here, pure, slightly metallic.

"The water's delicious."

"It's from our own spring," says Gabriel. He tips the peas out of the colander into a large porcelain bowl. Stella appears in the doorway, she has changed into a pair of jeans and a white T-shirt. She still looks elegant, even though she's now barefoot.

"How's it going?" she says.

"Fine," says Gabriel. "I'm just going to put the cheese in the oven, then dinner will be ready."

We eat on the veranda. Stella has set the table beautifully with linen napkins that look old, and a large bunch of flowers in an old porcelain jug with a crackled glaze. Lupins, daisies, red clover. The clover is wilting slightly. It's just going over, but still has that intense, chilly redness.

"*Trifolium pratense*," Stella murmurs as she adjusts a drooping flower head.

"Bloody know-it-all." Gabriel smiles, his voice is kind, as if he's proud of her really. Stella knows the Latin names of all the plants, sometimes she doesn't even seem to be aware that she's saying them.

It's a little cooler now. Gabriel has made a starter of goat cheese on white bread and a salad decorated with marigolds. They taste peppery, and are delicious with honey drizzled over the cheese. As soon as I swallow the first bite I realize how hungry I am. I have to make a real effort not to gobble my food. Gabriel watches me as I pop a piece of cheese in my mouth and I immediately feel embarrassed, convinced that he will think I'm greedy.

"That was absolutely delicious," I say when I have finished chewing.

He nods.

"Good," he says in a matter-of-fact tone of voice, as if he already knew it was delicious and I have given the correct answer. At the same time he always seems to be on the verge of smiling, that's what I think as I listen to his conversation with Stella; he varies between sounding firm and smiling broadly at something she has said. It's difficult to tell when he's really serious and when he's just pretending.

"So how's university going?" says Stella, turning to me.

"Okay," I mumble.

I had hoped to avoid the question, but at the same time I knew it was inevitable. Stella raises her eyebrows.

"Okay?"

I have to finish chewing before I can answer. The sugar snap peas are crunchy, I haven't eaten them raw for such a long time, not for many years. We used to grow them in the kitchen garden at home when Stella and I were little, we were always so eager to pick them that we used to eat them up while the peas were no more than little granules in the pods. They suddenly feel stringy in my mouth. I swallow.

"I've still got a few points left from the spring semester. I haven't done my assignment yet."

Stella nods.

"Presumably you have to do that before the start of the fall semester?"

"Yes."

She nods again.

Stella shows me around after dinner. The sun is just going down, the house is surrounded by fields of crops and the horizon is far away in every direction. The sky is immense and still blue, although it is almost a lavender color now. There are plants growing everywhere, in pots and beds, clambering over walls and trellises, spreading across the ground. Nasturtiums tumble from an old zinc tub, a tangled, sprawling mass with shoots apparently sprouting at random in all directions, desperately searching for something to cling to.

The kitchen garden is over in the corner, full of herbs and vegetables, nervously trembling cosmos and the robust marigolds that were used to decorate the salad, and there are strawberries, just like we used to have in our kitchen garden back home. Stella and I used to run outside first thing in the morning during our summer holidays, barefoot and still in our night-dresses, to see if any strawberries had ripened since the previous evening. I can clearly remember that spe-cial feeling of an early summer morning, that freshly washed smell, the chilly dew on the lawn making the blades of grass stick to the soles of our feet. Stella lifts the leaves of a strawberry plant to show me the ber-ries, which are tiny. The plants have been growing in the same spot for several years now, she explains, they will need to be moved next summer. There are no nutrients left in the soil.

The garden is full of wildflowers, farther away I can see clover and lupins and daisies and bright-orange lilies called tiger lilies.

"Old cottage garden flowers," says Stella, although the house could hardly be described as a cottage. She shows me hollyhocks and mint and hops that were planted long ago, a hundred years ago, maybe more. The house used to be a farmhouse once upon a time, it has been rebuilt and extended since then, the land rented out, the barn torn down, the former henhouse converted into a toolshed. Next to the shed stands an old greenhouse. Behind it the grass is tall, and the garden ends in a stone wall, which is falling down. There are huge bluebells growing between the stones, Stella says there are snakes there, adders, she has seen them several times basking in the sun, she tells me to be careful.

"Gabriel's maternal grandparents used to live here," she tells me. "He inherited the place five years ago. It's beautiful, isn't it?"

I nod. We walk around the side of the house and Stella points up at the big glassed-in balcony.

"That's where he sits and works."

We go back inside, it's quiet, dark in the kitchen too by now. Stella shows me where I'm staying, a little guest room on the ground floor, pleasant in an impersonal way. The wooden floor is painted white, and on a chest of drawers there is a bunch of the same flowers we had on the table earlier. On the bed there is a beautifully crocheted bedspread, perhaps Gabriel's grandmother made it. A round, milk-white porcelain ceiling light spreads a warm glow.

"I must go to bed," Stella says. "I have to be at work early in the morning to prepare a planting scheme. If I'm not there to keep an eye on things, they usually go wrong."

She makes a face, then smiles.

"I'm glad you're here at last," she says in a more serious tone of voice.

"Me too," I say, noticing how my eyes are darting all over the place, glancing at Stella, then looking down at the floor. I fix my gaze on the pattern on an old rug, its colors faded.

"I can finish work a bit earlier tomorrow," she says. "We could do something together. Would you like to come into town?"

"Sure."

"I'll call you in the morning and we can sort something out," she says, and I nod.

"You ought to close the window when the light is on," she adds. "Otherwise the mosquitoes come in."

I go over to the window and lift the catch, it grates and squeaks. Stella smiles.

"Nothing works properly around here," she says.

"I think it's lovely."

Through the window I can see the front garden, the fruit trees like big dark shapes in the twilight.

"If you don't want to go to bed yet, Gabriel's bound to be up for a few hours."

She picks up a few crumpled scraps of a wilting red clover that have drifted down onto the chest of drawers and holds them in her hand.

"I hope you sleep well," she says, sounding both polite and slightly distant.

"I'm sure I will," I reply.

She gives me a hug, then goes out onto the veranda to say goodnight to Gabriel. I sit on the bed for a while thinking that I ought to unpack my bags, but I feel tired, slightly drowsy from the food and wine. I open my suitcase and take out a thin cardigan instead and put it on. It's not cold but it is cooler now, and when I step out onto the veranda it's growing dark. Gabriel has lit an old paraffin lamp that is standing on the table, the smell reminds me of something, something from when I was a child. He's sitting reading with a glass of wine beside him, he smiles when he sees me.

"All right?" he says. "How's the head?"

"Better, thanks. I don't think I'd had enough to drink, and then it was just so hot."

"Would you like some more wine?"

"Yes please, if you're having some."

"Go and get yourself a clean glass then—I expect Stella has already put the other one in the dishwasher."

I open the wrong cupboard doors in the kitchen twice before I find the wineglasses, there are several different ones, a few of each, and they all look old. Gabriel is just moving a speaker from the living room onto the veranda when I come back, he puts on a vinyl LP, which crackles as the needle lands on the surface of the record. I don't recognize the song, but I do recognize David Bowie's voice. Gabriel sits down beside me on the sofa and fills up my glass, I take a sip. It's the same wine we had with dinner, but it seems to me that it tastes different now, rougher.

"So how do you like living in Stockholm?" Gabriel asks.

"Not much, to be honest."

"Neither did I."

"You used to live in Stockholm?"

"Indeed I did. For quite a long time."

We talk about Stockholm for a while, and I tell him about the apartment I'm renting as a sublet, the very thought of it makes me feel slightly uncomfortable as I remember its particular level of oppressive stuffiness on sunny days. It's actually a lovely apartment, full of details I like: huge marble windowsills, a beautiful parquet floor, a view over pine trees, pine trees that I have begun to think of as functionalist suburban pine trees. I like the fact that they look a certain way, slightly weary after a long life in a residential area, kind of dry and dusty. When the sun shines the apartment feels dusty too, as if the air is standing still, as if everything is immediately covered in a thin film of dust which the sun suddenly reveals, sometimes I think it's hard to breathe, and I have to push all the windows wide open, go and stand outside on the balcony.

"You and Stella haven't seen each other for quite a while, have you?" says Gabriel.

"Not since Christmas."

He nods.

"Do you think it was stupid of her to move out here?"

"No, I mean she got a job here, so . . ."

A small smile plays around his lips.

"But I'm too old for her—isn't that what everyone says?"

"No . . ." I mumble. "Not that I've heard."

He changes the subject, much to my relief. Because I actually have heard people say that Gabriel is too old for Stella, I've heard my mother and father say it, and I've seen relatives raise their eyebrows, meaning exactly that. He's at least forty-five, which means there must be fifteen years between them, maybe more. I remember when Stella first told our parents about him, it was at Easter two years ago, we were eating at the dining table in the living room, daffodils on the table and lots of food, we'd been working together in the kitchen all day, Mom and Stella and I. Easter was early that year, and outside everything was cold and gray. The memory has wrapped itself around the Easter celebrations like an unpleasant membrane, I thought about it last Easter too, felt the atmosphere around the table was stiff even though Stella wasn't there, or maybe that was the reason why. She hadn't known Gabriel for very long when she told us about him, in fact she had just finished with Erik, her former boy-friend, he was supposed to have been joining us for Easter, it had all been arranged ages ago. My mother and father couldn't understand Stella at all when she said she was no longer in love with Erik, that particular line of reasoning didn't work with them. They said he was always so kind to her, they talked about the apart-ment, the fantastic condo he'd bought, Stella had only just moved in. Stella said again that she was no longer in love with him, that she hadn't been for quite some time. My mother asked what Stella was intending to do about all the practicalities: where was she going to live, how was she going to support herself? Stella screamed at her, that hadn't happened for ages, not since Stella was living at home. When Mom started to cry, Stella left the table. I still hate thinking about it.

"You're not really alike," says Gabriel. "You and Stella."

"She's more like Mom. Both in her appearance and in her ways."

"And you're like your dad?"

"Yes, or our grandmother when she was young . . . and our aunts."

Gabriel looks as if he's about to say something, but changes his mind. Instead he tops off my glass.

"So what is it you do in Stockholm?" he asks. "What are you studying?"

"The history of art."

"And you've got an assignment to do? What's it about?"

I shrug my shoulders.

"I'm not really sure yet, but something to do with Dante Gabriel Rossetti, I think. The literary themes in his paintings, perhaps. But I haven't quite decided."

He nods, smiles at me.

"Good choice."

I smile back.

"What else?" he says. "Job?"

"No."

"Boyfriend?"

"Yes."

He nods again, smiling as if he's expecting me to tell him more.

"His name is Peter . . ." I begin. Gabriel is still smiling, and so am I, although I do feel slightly embarrassed at the same time, it's the expression on his face, it's hard to read his reaction to the simplest facts.

"Didn't he want to come with you?" says Gabriel.

I shake my head.

"No, he's in Spain at the moment. With some friends."

"I see."

I like the way he says that, making a simple statement, as if he understands exactly what is behind the information that Peter is on holiday without me, and there is no need for me to say any more on the subject.

The black cat appears on the veranda, Gabriel entices it over and pats the sofa with his hand. It jumps up and settles down, giving every appearance of falling asleep instantly. It's called Nils, says Gabriel, it used to belong to his grandmother. Then he starts to tell me a complicated story about someone he used to study with in Stockholm who lived in the same part of the city as me, I'm laughing, we're both laughing. Suddenly Stella is standing in the doorway with a cardigan over her nightdress.

"Could you turn the music down a little?" she says. "I need to get some sleep."

Her tone of voice is pleasant, but I can sense an underlying irritation. Stella isn't as good at hiding her feelings as she thinks she is, I realized that a long time ago. I wonder if Gabriel has realized it too.

"Of course," he says. "Sorry, darling."

I get up from the sofa.

"I think I'll head off to bed as well," I say.

"Lightweights," Gabriel mutters, but with a smile. "In that case maybe I'll try to work for a little while."

———

When Stella calls I'm up, busy hanging my clothes in the closet in the spare room. I let the phone ring for some time before I realize that Gabriel is either asleep or working, and isn't going to answer.

"That took a hell of a long time," says Stella. She sounds stressed.

"I didn't know whether to answer it or not."

"Did you sleep well? It wasn't too hot?"

"No, it was fine."

"Do you still fancy coming into town this afternoon?"

"Yes, of course."

She starts to give me instructions about what time the bus goes and where we are to meet, then she says she has to sort something out and brings the conversation to an abrupt end. I eat breakfast on the veranda while leafing through a copy of *Dagens Nyheter* that I've found in the kitchen, it's thin and flimsy, as if there's a shortage of news today. I wonder whether it was Gabriel or Stella who brought the newspaper in, whether Gabriel has already woken up and had breakfast and sat down at his desk on the glassed-in balcony to work, or whether he's still asleep up there. The house is silent, it's just as hot again today. It occurs to me that I ought to put on a dress instead of my jeans, but I'm so pale and I don't want to show my legs yet. Stella has a perfect soft golden tan, she's spent a lot of time outside this summer even though she hasn't had any holiday yet. She's been working outdoors, and has spent the weekends in the garden.

She looked so fresh in her light summer clothes yesterday, she always looks fresh, even in her working clothes; she usually wears an old men's shirt and jeans and puts her hair up, she looks like something from a fashion magazine even when she's digging.

She works for the local council in the parks and gardens department, it's her job to decide which flowers should be planted in which containers around the town, which shrubs in which beds, when and how the trees should be pruned, and where to put the Christmas lights in December. She is the youngest person ever to hold this post, and the first woman as well, my parents usually mention this with great pride whenever they are talking to anyone about her.

She is waiting for me at the bus depot next to the train station.

"God, it's so hot," is the first thing she says. "How can you stand wearing those?"

She nods in the direction of my jeans.

"I'm fine."

"Shall we see if we can find you a skirt?"

"No."

"Why not?"

I sigh, suddenly remembering how stubborn she can be, even though she doesn't appear to notice it herself.

"I've brought a dress with me, I just didn't want to wear it today, that's all."

She nods and seems to give in. We wander around the town center for a while, in silence at first, but then Stella starts to point out the planting she was responsible for this morning, showing me some concrete containers filled with lavender and some other purple flowers I don't know the name of. She looks pleased when I say they look lovely. She stops outside a café.

"Shall we have a coffee?"

She looks at me.

"Sure."

Stella chooses a table in the shade and asks the waitress for a mineral water and a coffee. I'm hungry, and when I realize Stella is paying I order a sandwich.

"Have you spoken to Gabriel today?" she wonders.

"No, I didn't want to go upstairs in case I might be disturbing him."

She nods, leans back in her chair, and pushes her sunglasses up onto her forehead, her pupils contracting even though we're sitting in the shade. Our eyes are the same color, a grayish blue which is difficult to put a name to. Although we're not particularly alike, I think our eyes are.

Stella clears her throat.

"So how are things with Peter?" she asks.

I don't know if she's asking how he is, or how things are between the two of us, but it doesn't really matter because I don't know anyway.

"I don't know."

She looks at me in surprise, almost annoyed, as if she hadn't expected an honest answer.

"He's in Spain with some friends."

"Without you?"

I shrug my shoulders. I don't want to talk about Peter, I've been thinking how nice it is that he's barely crossed my mind since I came here. Stella seems to understand.

"I thought we could do some shopping before we go home," she says instead. "Anything in particular you'd like for dinner?"

"Not really."

"Gabriel does a wonderful grilled salmon, it's absolutely delicious. He uses a secret marinade."

She smiles, I nod.

"We could do some potatoes in a dill sauce to go with it," she adds. "Dill grows like a weed in our garden, we could make enough dill sauce for everything."

She picks up her bag, pulls down her sunglasses.

"Right then. Off we go."

⁓

I'm alone in the house. Gabriel has gone into town with Stella to do some shopping and go to the bank.

It's almost eleven thirty when I wake up. I haven't slept well even though I've slept late, in fact I haven't slept well since I arrived. It's an uneasy sleep, I wake up several times during the night, and in between I sleep so deeply that I feel disorientated when I do wake up. I think I start to dream as soon as I get into bed and close my eyes. The air in the room is bad, even though I keep the windows open all day and all evening; I think maybe there's something in the walls, or in the foundations. Mold, something wrong.

The weather is still relentlessly beautiful. I take a long shower, even though Stella has asked me to be careful with the amount of water I use. The bathroom mirror is misty with condensation, I wipe it with the palm of my hand and contemplate my face. It looks somehow strange, as if my features are too round, too weak, as if they are in the process of disintegrating. Stella and I are different in that way, everything about her face is sharper, clearer, and I have always thought it makes her look more refined, more elegant, more intelligent. I stare at my mouth, thinking that my lips look swollen, fleshy, in a way that is vulgar, almost disgusting.

I take a stroll around the garden to dry my hair in the sun. It's too hot for jeans now, the heat has forced me to put on the only dress I have with me, and I glance down at my legs, my feet in the grass. I look pale. This is the first time in ages I've gone barefoot.

Bumblebees are buzzing among small flowers on the lawn, and I take great care not to step on any of them. Once, a long time ago, possibly on the last occasion when I walked barefoot on grass, I happened to step on a fallen apple with a wasp inside it. We were playing croquet in the garden at my parents' house, it was when Stella was still with Erik, so it was Stella and Erik and me. Stella was winning when I stood on the wasp and we had to stop playing. I can still feel the stabbing pain in my foot at the memory, and I can hear Stella's voice in my head, she kept on saying "It's fine, it's only a wasp sting," but my foot swelled up and in the end I started to cry. At that point she gave up, and she and Erik drove me to primary care. The doctor said I was probably particularly sensitive to insect bites and stings.

I go indoors, wandering aimlessly through the living room and back out into the hallway, upstairs to the first floor, through Stella and Gabriel's bedroom and onto the glassed-in balcony where Gabriel has his desk. It is old and made of dark wood, it looks heavy and is cluttered with books and piles of paper and several blue-and-white china cups with dried coffee dregs in the bottom. Balanced on a heap of old newspapers is an overfilled mosaic ashtray in shades of turquoise, with a brass dolphin leaping up from a foaming wave. It makes me smile, it's just so kitsch.

In a terra-cotta pot on the floor there's an enormous angel's trumpet, the flowers will be out soon, and the swollen buds look like big green pupae with something trying to force its way out. A number of postcards are pinned up on a pillar between two windows: Hokusai's *The Great Wave*, a hollow-eyed Madonna by Munch, one of Rossetti's red-haired women— Gabriel and I are equally taken with them. On the windowsill below lie several dead flies. It's warm and damp like the inside of a greenhouse, little drops of water trickle slowly down the inside of the panes of glass.

Gabriel has left his computer on. A blue cube is spinning around on the screen, slowly changing into a sphere. I move the mouse a fraction to remove the screen saver, and a Word document appears. I glance over my shoulder, an instinctive movement to check that no one is watching me. Then I perch on the very edge of the chair, which looks as old as the desk, it's an office chair with wheels and slats across the back and a seat made of dark-green leather held in place by small copper upholstery nails. Only two lines of text are visible on the screen, it looks like the end of a poem: "floats very slowly, lying in her long veils /—In the far-off woods you can hear the call of the hunters." I don't recognize the words and am about to scroll up the page when I hear the muffled sound of a car door closing. I stiffen for a moment, then get up so quickly that I almost tip over the chair, one of the arms hits me hard on the thigh, and I just have time to think that I'm going to have a bruise. I have to activate the screen saver again, I click on the desktop, properties, screen saver, what's it called, the cube that turns into a sphere? I realize I'm not going to have time to apply it, I can already hear the crunch of footsteps on the gravel path and I hurry through the bedroom and try to calm myself before setting off down the stairs. At that very moment the door opens and Gabriel steps into the hallway, his hands full of shopping bags, the bamboo curtain dancing merrily behind him. He looks at me.

"Hi there," he says, sounding slightly surprised.

"Hi."

I smile at him.

"What are you doing?" he asks.

"I was looking for Nils."

"He's outside. I've just seen him in the flower bed at the front."

I nod, he carries on looking at me, puts the bags down on the floor.

"How was town?" I say.

"Good, it was nice to see a few people. How are you—you look a bit pale?"

I raise my hand to my forehead in a pure reflex action.

"I've got a slight headache," I say. "I think it's the heat."

I am tired of my pale body, which feels like Stockholm's last hold on me, the proof that I have spent far too much time indoors instead of having fun. I have dragged one of the chairs from the patio onto the lawn, which is in sunlight all day. A bikini would be too embarrassing, I'm still too pale, I don't want to show that much flesh. Wearing a pair of short shorts and a tank top feels sufficiently undressed, and after I have been sitting in the sun for a while I feel a little braver and pull up my top slightly, exposing my stomach to the sun. Behind me the last of the roses are flowering in the borders, along with lavender and Sweet William. A small currant bush is weighed down by the heavy bunches of shiny red berries, I have eaten a few, it must be just as long since I last ate them as when I last ate sugar snap peas, and yet the taste was completely familiar, as if it had been only yesterday. I like redcurrants even though they taste of little more than sourness, I like the consistency, the sensation of crushing a berry in my mouth, biting through the skin and feeling all the rough little seeds dispersing.

I fall asleep in the sun, when I wake up I look at my watch straightaway and realize I have slept for almost half an hour. The clouds that were in the sky when I sat down on the lawn have completely disappeared, and instead the sky is open and blue, everything I can see has a surreal sharpness. Even in the distance, on the horizon beyond the fields, the perspective does not blur land and sky into a pale-blue mist. It's the same with the smells. Sharp, acrid, as if there is absolutely no resistance to them in the air. As soon as I wake I am aware of the clean, chemical smell of paint. It is obtrusive and cold, as if it wants to be inhaled, and I obey, avidly drawing it into my lungs. I have always liked those pungent aromas: the smell in the garage, gas and exhaust fumes, the smell of thick black felt-tip pens, turpentine, glue, it smells like Dad, I think to myself, and I suddenly realize that all my memories of smells like this are linked to him. We were painting my room together once, I must have been about twelve or thirteen, just between junior high and high school, I suddenly decided that everything in my room that I hadn't chosen for myself was hopelessly childish. I wanted everything that was pink painted white, and Dad and I were going to do it together. I remember the tin of white paint, the strong smell filling the entire room, I remember lying down on the bed, closing my eyes and inhaling the acrid smell, feeling slightly dizzy as my cheeks grew warm, I almost felt drunk even though I didn't realize it at the time. I remember thinking it probably wasn't a good idea to breathe in the paint fumes, but I liked doing it anyway.

I close my eyes now, thinking that such a pure smell has to come from white paint, the whitest of white, almost fluorescent, like white under ultraviolet light. But this paint is actually a grubby Falun red, Gabriel is painting the old henhouse where Stella keeps her garden tools, along with a whole lot of clutter that has been in there for fifty years, maybe a hundred, maybe more. I watch him from a distance, he looks as if he is concentrating hard, and I imagine that he is not thinking about the painting at all, but about something else. I watch him until I begin to feel ashamed of spying on him, then I go over to speak to him.

"Gabriel?"

He jumps and turns around.

"You gave me a fright."

He looks almost embarrassed, as if he has been somehow caught out.

"Sorry, I didn't mean to."

"It's okay." He smiles. "How are you?"

"Fine . . . except I fell asleep in the sun. I'm afraid I might have burnt myself."

He gazes at me, looking at parts of my body that are not covered by clothes: my arms and legs, a quick glance at the low neckline of my top.

"Do you feel as if you have?" he says.

I am slightly embarrassed by his scrutiny, I imagine he must think I look pale, wrong in some way, ugly. But that is not what his expression suggests. I wonder what he's thinking.

A lock of hair has fallen into his eyes, he pushes it back with his hand and gets a red mark on his forehead. When he looks at his hand and sees that it is sticky with paint, he realizes what has happened.

"Have I got red paint on my forehead?"

"Yes."

I smile. So does he, slightly embarrassed again.

"A lot?"

"No, not really . . . let me."

I move a step closer and run my thumb gently over the mark on his forehead. He looks at me, no longer smiling. There is a strong smell of paint, as if the hot, still air is intensifying the smell, making it linger. The lock of hair falls into his eyes again, and I gently push it aside to get at the paint. I can feel his breath against my cheek, he is close now, bending his head toward me so that I can reach. His forehead is brown from the sun, his whole face, his arms, he is wearing a faded black T-shirt and he smells wonderful, warm.

"Has it gone?"

"Yes."

I hold up my hand to show him, red paint on my thumb and forefinger, and he suddenly grabs hold of my wrist, twists my hand around, and looks at my fingers. It is a rapid movement, decisive, his grip is hard, just like when I met him on that first evening, the firm handshake. Perhaps he isn't aware of how strong he is.

"Pretty nail polish," he says.

I did my nails last night, a cool pink, shimmering like mother-of-pearl in the sunlight.

"Thanks," I say quietly.

My cheeks flush red. He lets go of my hand and smiles at me.

"I think there's a bottle of white spirit under the sink," he says. "If you want to get the paint off."

I rub my thumb and forefinger together, the red pigment in the paint adhering to the fine lines on my fingertips so that the pattern on them stands out, they look like the rings on a tree trunk.

"No, it's fine. I wondered if there was anything I could do. Cut the grass maybe? Stella said it needed doing."

"I was going to do it this evening."

"I'd be happy to do it."

"There's no need."

The grass really is too long. I realize cutting it will be hard work, it's a big garden, and Gabriel doesn't even have a normal lawn mower, just an old manual one that belonged to his grandfather. I remember Stella saying that Gabriel can't stand things that make a loud noise.

"I feel as if I ought to be doing something to help," I say. "I mean, I'm doing nothing."

"Perhaps you could start working on your assignment?"

I sigh and raise my eyebrows in a gesture of weariness, he smiles, his expression thoughtful as he gazes at me, his eyes lingering briefly on my legs before he quickly looks up and out across the fields toward the horizon.

"I have a suggestion," he says hesitantly. "If you really do want to help with something?"

"Absolutely."

"Come with me, then."

Up on the glassed-in balcony the computer is switched on, the screen saver's cube drifting indolently across the monitor. Gabriel presses a key and a Word document appears. He scrolls back to the beginning.

"Sit down."

He wheels out the old office chair and nods toward it.

One of the flowers on the angel's trumpet has come out. It's enormous and looks tropical, as if it doesn't belong here on the balcony at all but ought to be in a jungle somewhere. It gives off a sweet smell, it's as if the air is perfumed. I feel tired, I ought to drink more, you're supposed to drink a lot when it's this hot. Gabriel puts the big ashtray with the dolphin on the floor and opens one of the windows as I sit down on the chair.

There is a low bookcase along the wall at the back of the balcony. Piles of newspapers and magazines are balanced on top of it, along with heaps of papers, files, and books. The bottom shelf is filled by a long row of books with the same pale-gray spine. When Gabriel notices me looking at them, he bends down and takes one out. On the front cover is a picture of a woman lying in a pond, surrounded by flowers. When you have read the book, you know that she is dead. *Ophelia*, it says above the picture.

"Have you got a copy?" Gabriel asks.

"No."

He holds the book out to me.

"Here, take it. But don't read it now. The new one is much better."

He nods in the direction of the screen.

"I wondered if you could have a look at it for me? I'll print it out for you when I've bought a new ink cartridge, then you won't have to read it on the screen."

He leaves me at the desk, I hear him walking down the stairs. I look at the text on the screen. Stella hasn't read it, I know that, she told me she didn't even know what his new book was about, she said he doesn't seem to want to discuss his writing with her. I won't be able to tell her he's asked me to read it.

After a while I see Gabriel walking across the grass on his way back to the old henhouse. I think about his grip on my wrist, I can't get the thought out of my head. I close my eyes, replaying the scene in my mind: the way he takes a firm grip and twists my hand around to look at my nails, his hand holding tightly on to mine.

I watch him until he has painted his way around the corner of the shed and I can no longer see him. Then I begin to read.

Gabriel's first novel was published just after I started high school, a friend bought it and kept telling me I ought to read it, she lent it to me and I can still remember it lying on top of a pile of magazines next to my bed with its beautiful shiny cover. I read it quickly, the way I read most things in those days, a kind of binge reading aimed at getting through as many books as possible, shoveling down as many as I could in order to tick them off against a list in my head. Perhaps it was because I didn't have much else to do during those years; with a significant number of books behind me, I could at least feel as if I had used the time for something sensible. I have only vague memories of Gabriel's novel but I do remember that I liked it, I remember a cloying sense of love bordering on obsession that was so well written I felt as if I had experienced it myself.

I have been sitting at the computer for several hours when I hear the sound of Stella's car coming along the gravel road, I get up and take my copy of *Ophelia* downstairs, feeling slightly dizzy from staring at the screen for so long. Through the kitchen window I see Stella getting out of the car and waving to an elderly couple down the road, they wave back, she walks over and chats with them for a few minutes before they turn and head off in the direction from which they came. She's carrying a plastic bag holding two containers of strawberries when she comes into the kitchen.

"Have you read it?" is the first thing she says.

"What?" I say quickly, thinking that I sound defensive, caught out, but she doesn't seem to notice.

"Did he give you the book?"

She nods toward my hand.

"Oh, that. Yes, yes he did."

"I thought you'd read it before?"

"I have, but it was a long time ago. I can hardly remember anything about it."

"It's about his ex," says Stella.

"Is she dead?"

Stella laughs.

"Oh no. She dumped him."

"Oh?"

"He's not that easy to live with," she says quietly.

I am shocked by the sudden confidence, Stella almost looks surprised herself.

"Who were those people?" I say in order to break the tense silence that follows. "The people you were talking to?"

"Anders and Karin," she says, placing the strawberries on the draining board. "They're our closest neighbors, it's their house you can see on the other side of the field."

"What did they want?"

"They were just out for a walk."

"Along this road? But it ends here."

"They come by sometimes just to check things out. Make sure everything's okay."

"What do you mean, make sure everything's okay?"

"That's what people do in the country," she says, sounding slightly irritated. "When it's a long way between neighbors. You don't have a problem with that, do you?"

She looks at me, her expression challenging.

"No, of course not."

"What have you been doing today?" she goes on.

"Nothing special."

"Have you started working on your assignment?"

"No, not yet."

"Don't you think you should make a start soon?"

"Yes."

She nods, looking stern. She can still make me feel like a child. Just like when I failed at something when I was little and she was disappointed in me; she couldn't hide it then either, she wore the same expression of reluctant indulgence.

"Did you bring in the mail?" she asks.

"I checked earlier, but there wasn't anything."

Stella looks cross.

"I'm waiting for some seeds," she says.

She sinks down on one of the kitchen chairs, she looks tired, she works too hard. The former head of parks and gardens was almost seventy when he retired, half senile, she's still trying to clear up after him, sort out the paperwork, the admin, the finances. She says she really needs an assistant, someone who could take care of all the paperwork so that she could concentrate on what she's trained to do, she hadn't realized the job would involve so much paperwork.

"He bought such horribly ugly containers," she says. "Great big plastic urns, I don't know what he was thinking of. Lots and lots of them. They're piled up in the cellar, huge towers of pots, they look like something you might see outside a pizzeria. And the sad thing is that there's a whole lot of old containers there too, big bowls made of iron or bronze or whatever it is . . . They've got grooves on the bottom, they're the color of lady's mantle, they've gone completely green with the verdigris, they must be from the last century. The trouble is I haven't got any money now, I'll have to wait until next year before I can do anything with them. At the moment I'll be happy if I can scrape together enough for a Christmas tree to go in the square."

She gives a slightly weary smile.

"Perhaps we could have lunch together one day?" she suggests. "It would make a change for you, instead of hanging around here all the time."

For once I find it difficult to work out whether she's simply being kind or there's something else underlying her words.

"I like being here," I say, watching her face and hoping for a reaction, a furrow in her brow, something, but her expression remains pleasant, smiling. "But I'd love to meet you for lunch."

⸻

Gabriel and I are sitting on the patio in the evening, we've done this almost every night since I arrived, he and I, Stella goes to bed early. We're both going to read, we've each got a book with us, I've chosen one at random from the bookcase in the living room because I like the title. The living room is almost like a library; all of Gabriel's grandparents' books and all of his, shelf after shelf covering the walls, apart from one wall that is covered in pictures from floor to ceiling— Japanese woodcuts, quiet Skåne landscapes, a portrait of a woman in a red sweater behind a still life of a bowl of fruit, that's Gabriel's grandmother when she was young in the 1930s, painted by someone who is obviously well-known but whose name I have never heard, a friend of the family.

There is a full moon tonight, we have watched it move across the vast sky, it is a harvest moon, burning orange-yellow above the fields of ripe corn. Gabriel is flicking through a book too, although we're not really reading, either of us. A quarter of an hour passes, perhaps half an hour, then Gabriel brings the speaker out of the living room. He lets me choose a record on alternate evenings, tonight it's his turn. We keep the volume low, Stella sleeps with her window open. We keep our voices low too, almost whispering sometimes, so that we won't wake her. Gabriel does most of the talking, telling stories about people he knows or has known, gossiping about authors and journalists. I've never even heard of half of them, but he explains patiently, getting up to fetch books from the living room, showing me photos of the authors inside the covers and telling me about various intrigues. It's mostly to do with love affairs, infidelity and scandal, or quarrels, usually about work, about different appointments, slander behind people's backs, or even quite openly; people who seem prepared to sacrifice just about anything for the sake of their careers.

Gabriel was out and about a lot after his last novel was published, it was a great success, the newspapers wrote about him, he appeared on the sofa on a number of TV programs, went to all the parties, knew everyone in Stockholm. These days he is in contact with hardly anyone from those days, he looks sad as he tells me this. His new novel was actually completed several years ago, but his publishers weren't satisfied and wanted him to make some changes, and he ended up rewriting the whole thing. He's almost finished it now but he isn't happy with it at all, he'd really like to rewrite it all over again but it's impossible, it would never be finished if he did that. He looks sad when he tells me this too.

I tell him how much my friend and I liked *Ophelia*, and that I loved the photo of him inside the front cover, a black-and-white picture of a young Gabriel leaning against a birch tree, it looks like late spring, the leaves on the tree are still small enough to let through plenty of light, the dappled, impressionistic light of late spring. Gabriel is wearing a black jacket and a white shirt, he is holding a cigarette in his hand and looking straight into the camera. I thought he looked so worldly, so unattainable.

He laughs, tells me I'm sweet. Stella hadn't read any of his books when they met, he says. She hardly even knew who he was. They met at a party while she was still a student, he tells me how beautiful he thought she was, pale skin and strawberry-blonde hair, I swallow, I have to look away, gaze at the moon, which has moved a little farther across the sky, it just seems to be getting bigger and bigger. Stella was wearing a white cardigan, he says, and I know the one he means, I envied her that cardigan. She wore it one Christmas at Mom and Dad's, white angora, she had her hair up and she looked both severe and soft at the same time in her silky cardigan, she looked like someone I would never have dared to talk to if she hadn't been my sister. I tell him this and he laughs again, says he wouldn't have had the nerve either if he hadn't been drinking, he says she looked so young, he is watching me over the rim of his glass, seems on the verge of saying something more, but changes his mind.

He is already sitting on the patio when I wake up, reading the newspaper with his feet on the table, a blue-and-white coffee cup beside them. The clear air has become misty, but the heat has not diminished. It is different now, sultry and oppressive, as if a thunderstorm is coming. Swallows swoop across the grass, their movements rapid and erratic, flickering. They are flying low now, the approaching storm means the insects they are hunting stay close to the ground, it's to do with the air pressure, it forces them downward, Stella has explained it to me. My head feels fragile, as if a headache is just coming to life deep inside and will soon make its presence felt, sending out crackling impulses of pain that will thud against my forehead and my temples, as if I were inside a thunder ball. I think I ought to take a painkiller just to be on the safe side, I think about the cool rustle of the foil inside the box of tablets.

"I was going to cut the grass but I haven't got the energy in this heat," says Gabriel. "There's coffee in the machine if you want some."

When I come back with my coffee and a sandwich he passes me a section of the newspaper. I open it but can't be bothered to read anything, instead I watch Gabriel, who is half hidden behind his section, he's wearing a T-shirt today as well, I stare at his sunburnt arms. He puts the paper down on the table, quickly looks up at me, I meet his eyes and smile, he smiles back, glances distractedly at the recipe of the day on the back page, smoked mackerel with some kind of cold sauce. Then he pushes the newspaper away.

"So . . . what about going for a swim?"

"Sure . . . but where?"

He shrugs his shoulders.

"Wherever you like. There's a lake, it's about ten minutes' walk from here. Or we could drive to the sea. It's not very far."

"The sea sounds fantastic."

He gets to his feet.

"I'll go and get some towels."

All the plants in the garden have been affected by the heat. The orange nasturtiums are hanging their heads and looking limp. There's a water shortage, you're not really supposed to water the garden, but Stella does the rounds with her big watering can every evening anyway. She has taught me that you shouldn't water during the day, because the water evaporates straightaway, before it's had a chance to get beyond the surface, and it does no good. I'd still like to give the weary nasturtiums a good shower.

When I look closer I can see that the undersides of the leaves are covered in aphids, great black clumps of them, they are on the stems bearing the flower heads too, covering them completely so that the stems look thick and black, uneven. The more I look, the more aphids I see. In the end I almost believe they're multiplying before my very eyes, that the clumps on the underside of the leaves are slowly swelling, expanding. I turn away in disgust.

Gabriel hands me a towel.

"There's blackfly on the nasturtiums," I say.

"Happens every year."

The car is as hot as a sauna. The sun has been shining on the seats and they burn my thighs through my skirt, it smells of hot plastic, stuffy. When Gabriel turns the key, nothing happens. He tries several times, but the car refuses to start.

"What the fuck?" he mumbles crossly.

After at least fifteen attempts he gives up, leaves the keys dangling in the ignition and leans back in his seat with a resigned expression.

"Shall we walk to the lake instead?" I say.

He looks at me, gazes at me for several seconds, but doesn't reply. I look him straight in the eye, I haven't thought about the color of his eyes before, it's difficult to tell what it is. I hear him take a deep breath, then he leans over, places a hand behind my head, pulls me firmly toward him and kisses me. His kiss is also firm, he nearly forces my lips apart, hungrily, and I allow him to do it, I let his tongue into my mouth, he tastes of coffee and he smells good this time too, the same smell as when I wiped the paint off his forehead. I put my arms around him. He is breathing heavily now, I feel his hand through the fabric of my dress, feel it move across my back and I shudder with pleasure, press myself closer to him. Then he stops himself, places a hand on his forehead, looks almost tormented. His face is shiny, it must be 100 degrees in the car, 110, maybe more.

"We . . ." he begins, but breaks off.

He opens the door and gets out, running his hand through his hair.

"I'll call Anders and see if he's got time to come and take a look at the car."

"Okay," I say.

Gabriel is halfway up the path now, walking quickly. I open my door and realize my legs are shaking as I put my feet on the gravel next to the car. He stops and turns around.

"It's not difficult to find your way to the lake if you want a swim," he says. "You just follow the gravel road, then there's a path through the forest on the right, maybe five minutes away. You can't miss it."

"Okay," I say again.

Gabriel disappears into the house. I take my towel and set off toward the road.

It's a small lake, the trees around it are tall and straight and the water looks black from a distance, but it's actually yellowish and quite warm. There's a little sandy beach, but the sand gives way beneath my feet and I can tell there is mud underneath, a thin layer of pale sand on top of thick black mud. Perhaps that's what quicksand feels like, I think, and I am afraid to stand in the same spot for too long, afraid that the ground will give way beneath my feet, trapping me, dragging me down. There isn't a soul in sight, everything is still and silent apart from a bird repeating its long, drawn-out scream, I wonder what it might be, a black-throated diver perhaps, I'm really bad at recognizing bird calls. It sounds horrible. I'm sure there must be crayfish in the lake, I can see them in my mind's eye, their black shapes crawling along the bottom, big clumps of them, like the blackfly.

We learned to swim quite late, Stella and I. Somehow it seemed to me that I would never need to know how to do it, and I think Stella felt the same way. Every holiday when we were little we went to some cottage by the sea, to sandy Swedish beaches shelving gently into the water, saltspray roses in full bloom, stranded jellyfish, coarse gray-green grass and the sand at the water's edge, solid and compacted, sometimes etched with grooves from the waves in a way that seemed too good to be true, unnatural, as if someone had raked the entire shoreline just like the gravel path outside the church where we had our end-of-semester celebrations. We would sit on the sand right at the water's edge, where the water is at its warmest, we would walk around with our hands on the bottom, like crocodiles in tepid water, we would play ball and jump in the waves, but I never remember us swimming, I don't remember Stella swimming even though she was so much older than me. Swimming lessons in school were one long torment, everyone else had already learned to swim during the summer holidays and I ended up paddling around clumsily with a float around my waist, like two great big external orange lungs on my back. I hated the pungent smell of chlorine, and the swimming pool was ugly, I could feel it very clearly even if I was unable to put it into words at the time: water was not my element. I learned to swim eventually, the last in the class and very reluctantly, but I still don't enjoy it. I don't know how Stella feels, we haven't talked about it for years.

It is with a mixture of fear and pleasure that I close my eyes and sink beneath the surface of the water. I have that same strong feeling now, that I don't belong in the water, but I think that perhaps it can be changed, perhaps I can become someone else. Perhaps it's already happening. Even though the water is warm, almost too warm, it feels cool against my face. I think about Gabriel's kiss, his firm hand behind my head, on the back of my neck. When I open my eyes underwater my hands look white in the yellowness, my nail polish looks orange, it looks grubby, dirty. I lie on my back instead, feeling my hair float out across the water around my face. A few black alder cones are bobbing on the surface of the water a short distance away, and a dragonfly darts just above, its movements jerky.

I could drown and die here and nobody would notice, I think to myself, they would have to drag the lake for my body, they would find it down in the mud. I wonder if there are eels here, eels are scavengers, they eat people who have drowned. I daren't push my feet too far down for fear of touching something disgusting on the bottom, down there where the water is chilly. The alders are standing in a row on the shoreline, the sand has been washed away from around their roots, they are black and slippery, like black snakes reaching down into the water, I hurry out, suddenly convinced that the yellow water smells fetid. I jump as one of my wet curls tickles my shoulder, tumbling down my back, I quickly wrap the towel around my head, trapping them. The alders are reflected in the surface of the water, standing dark and silent in a row along the shoreline, there isn't a sound.

I don't have a change of clothes with me, and have to pull on my dress over my wet swimsuit. Do they usually come here to swim? I wonder. Stella and

Gabriel. Does he pull her toward him in the same way, forcing her lips apart, pressing himself against her? You could do anything here, no one would see. What would we have done if he had come with me? The thought excites me, his hands on my body, warm against my skin, which is covered in gooseflesh after my swim, one hand fastened around my wrist in a firm grip, the other hand under my dress, touching my thigh. I close my eyes. I would let him do anything he wants, I think, and am instantly surprised by my own thought, but yes, I think it again. Anything he wants, anything at all.

Stella and Gabriel are standing next to Gabriel's car when I get back, I recognize the neighbor Anders, who is leaning over the engine, looking concerned. Gabriel is wearing the same expression. Anders nods to me as I pass by.

"There's something wrong with the engine," says Stella.

"Oh right, that's not good."

Gabriel doesn't look at me. Stella follows me into the house.

"Was the water warm?" she wonders.

"It sure was."

"It usually is, it's so shallow."

"Do you know if there are any crayfish?"

"What?"

"In the lake."

"Oh . . . no, I don't think so."

"What about eels?"

Stella smiles.

"I don't know, ask Gabriel. Are you thinking of going fishing?"

"No, I just wondered."

We eat in silence, it's late, it's growing dark outside. Stella has lit the paraffin lamp on the veranda. Gabriel has barbecued some meat, fillet of beef, it's red in the center and has been cooked in one piece, lying there on the barbecue like a long, thick sausage. I am having difficulty eating it. They haven't sorted out the car, someone is coming to pick it up tomorrow to take it to a repair shop.

"The water lilies should be flowering now," says Stella. "Did you see them?"

It's a few seconds before I realize she's talking to me.

"Oh, in the lake?"

"Yes, in the lake."

She sounds annoyed and makes no attempt to hide it. She was complaining about a headache earlier, and about the heat. I know she's worried about the car too, that it will be expensive, that things are going to be difficult while it's being fixed. If Gabriel can't get around she will have to give him lifts, and she's the one who will have to do all the shopping and so on until it's back.

"No . . . I didn't see any water lilies."

"Maybe you just didn't notice them."

"I would have."

"Maybe you just didn't notice them," she repeats.

"There were no water lilies."

"There must have been. There are lots of them. *Nymphaea alba*. Oh, by the way—do you know if there are any crayfish in the lake?"

She turns to Gabriel.

"Not that I know of."

I think of the water lilies, of their roots down on the bottom of the lake, sunk in the mud, sending their shoots up toward the surface like distress flares. It must be unpleasant to swim among water lilies, their stems around your legs, winding around your calves and thighs. Water lily roots and eels, that's what is at the bottom of the lake. I poke at my meat, I can't eat any more.

"No good?"

Gabriel looks at me for the first time the entire evening.

"Oh, yes . . . it's just that I have a bit of a problem with red meat, that's all."

. . .

The thunderstorm does not come, it is still just as hot when I go to bed. My window is ajar, fixed with the catch, I would really like to open it wider but I don't feel all that safe, since I'm on the ground floor. Someone could get in, or something—an animal. It might not make any difference if I opened the window anyway, the air is still, it hangs heavy and dead, just as sultry as it was this afternoon, the only difference is that it's darker now.

I am just falling asleep when I hear noises from upstairs. Long, drawn-out sobs, I recognize them. Stella is crying, heartrending weeping, I can hear her gasping for breath, in my mind's eye I can see her whole body shaking. Then I hear the muted sound of Gabriel's voice, I can't hear what he's saying but from his tone it's obvious that he's angry but is controlling himself, then Stella's voice, a note of accusation. I pull the covers over my head, try not to listen. When I close my eyes beneath the covers my thoughts race back and forth inside my head, replaying the kiss in the car over and over again. I did nothing to encourage him, I think. I only looked at him, he was the one who kissed me. He shouldn't have done it, I shouldn't have let him, I should have pushed him away. Immediately the thought of his hand gripping my wrist is there again. Imagine if I had tried to push him away and he had stopped me, locking my hand with his, pushing himself against me, holding on to me. I wouldn't have been able to do anything to stop him. I try to push away the thought but it forces its way back, in the end I almost believe that's what really happened, it's like in the mornings sometimes when I'm really tired and instead of getting up I imagine I'm doing it, I lie there half asleep and imagine so vividly that I'm getting up and going into the bathroom that I'm surprised when I do wake up and realize I'm still lying in bed.

I must have fallen asleep properly then because I am woken by a scream, shrill and long drawn-out. My first thought is that it's Stella. That he has told her, that he felt bad, had to confess. I feel empty inside as I imagine hearing her footsteps on the stairs at any moment, what will she say to me? Or yell at me? I hear my own voice inside my head: "I didn't want to say anything to you, but he held me so I couldn't move, I couldn't do anything, he held my hands so I couldn't move and he kissed me." I'm good at lying, good at hitting the right tone of voice, good at convincing myself that what I'm saying is actually true, that's why it sounds so natural when I say it. It is almost true now. "I didn't know what was happening until he kissed me."

Then I realize the sound I've heard didn't come from upstairs but from outside, from the garden. I think it must be a cat, Nils is out at night and there are other cats around here, cats that don't belong to anyone, cats that have been left behind by summer visitors or cats from some of the farms in the area. They hunt at night, there are plenty of mice here, the house is old, and then there are all the crops, ripe yellow fields in all directions, and the old barns where the grain is stored. In my mind's eye I can see the mouse shrieking, it's one of the tiny ones that live under the house, I've seen one, little dark eyes like peppercorns, I can see it in the clutches of a cat, fighting for its life, screaming, twisting and turning, its heart beating in a panic as the cat sinks its teeth into the small body.

I switch on the bedside lamp and several moths that have been attracted by the light begin to dance around it as I pad across the white-painted wooden floor and close the window, drawing the thin curtains. I can hear a different sound now, muffled at first but quickly growing louder, sighs and whimpers, I quickly get back into bed, turn off the light. It isn't a cat this time, it's coming from upstairs again and I realize it's Stella, it's hard to work out if she is experiencing pain or pleasure, it's just on the borderline. I try to imagine what Gabriel is doing to her to make her sound like that, how he is touching her; the sounds she is making grow louder, faster. I close my eyes, thinking of his hands on the nape of my neck, the violence of his kiss, his hands moving across my back, his breathing heavy and aroused, his hand sliding down across my bottom and my thighs, finding its way under my dress as the other hand closes around my wrist. I imagine the weight of his body on mine, imagine that I am the one he is kissing now, that he is pressing his body hard against mine, that those whimpering noises are mine.

The bus into town takes a different route this time, following narrow, winding roads past farms and whitewashed churches and little groups of houses where all the mailboxes are arranged in a long row by the roadside. No one gets on and no one gets off anywhere and it feels as if it is taking an eternity, it's hot and there's an unpleasant, stuffy smell on the bus. I make patterns with my fingertips in the upholstery, I draw a heart, rub it out, draw another one.

Stella looks annoyed when I get off.

"You're very late."

"The bus took this weird detour."

She looks at her watch.

"I have to be back at one fifteen, we've got a meeting."

We go to the same café as last time, Stella orders a Caesar salad with a mineral water, I have the same.

The waitress gives a little smile when I say I'd like the same, glancing quickly from one to the other, I presume she thinks we're alike. Once when I was at junior high and Stella was at high school, a man in a department store asked if we were twins. I thought it was really funny, but Stella seemed annoyed more than anything when she explained that she was *much* older. She's always looked young, she still does, you could still take us for the same age if it weren't for her clothes, they're much more elegant than mine these days, they look more grown-up.

"It's good here," Stella says when the waitress returns with our salads. "Considering it's in a small town."

She smiles, perhaps with a hint of resignation. I know she misses Stockholm, she was much happier there than I have ever been, but she couldn't find a job. She was thinking of setting up her own business, helping rich people to design their gardens, but there's not much work available. You need contacts and she doesn't have any, no acquaintances who happen to know the acquaintances of the rich, or acquaintances of parents who might need to employ a garden designer.

"Was Gabriel awake when you left?"

"I didn't see him."

She sighs, pushes her sunglasses up onto her head, and leans closer to me across the table.

"I've been thinking about Erik lately," she says.

It's been such a long time since she mentioned Erik that I can't help looking surprised when she mentions his name, and she looks down, as if she thinks it sounded bad coming out of her mouth, as if she suspects that's what's going through my mind.

"And what have you been thinking?"

She shrugs her shoulders.

"Oh, I don't know . . ." she begins, then she clears her throat and suddenly sounds more sure of herself. "I've been thinking that things felt different with him. Safe, in a completely different way from how things are with . . . from how things are now."

"Do you mean it was better?"

"No," she says quickly, instinctively. Then she pauses and considers, twisting and turning her sunglasses in her hand. "I used to think it was boring. It was . . . stable. Gabriel is . . . well, things are more up and down now."

I nod. Perhaps this is only the beginning of a conversation. Perhaps she wants me to ask more questions, draw confidences out of her, I'm no good at that kind of thing. But I do wonder if there are problems between her and Gabriel, more serious problems than the occasional quarrel, than the fact that they're two moody individuals who can both get extremely angry. Problems that, even if they don't excuse something like kissing another person, might at least explain it.

When Stella puts her sunglasses back on I realize I've missed my chance to ask questions. Instead she starts talking about a girlfriend who's moved abroad, and then about her job, as usual.

"By the way, would you like to see the greenhouses?"

"What greenhouses?"

She grimaces slightly as if to indicate that I ought to know which greenhouses she means, but she looks amused rather than annoyed.

"The ones at work, of course."

She smiles, I nod.

"Sure."

Stella pays for lunch before we leave.

"Thanks," I say.

"You can treat me to lunch when you've got your own gallery," she says.

I laugh, the idea is just absurd, but although Stella is smiling she doesn't seem to be joking. It strikes me that her remarks about my assignment and the fact that I ought to study more are not just something she says in order to be difficult, but that she actually believes I could achieve something. I've never thought about it like that before. Suddenly I feel a rush of affection, just like when we were little and she would hold my hand when we were going somewhere and

I felt safe, certain that Stella could deal with absolutely anything, and the thought of Gabriel in the car makes me feel ashamed, I think once again that it wasn't my fault, but I should have protested, I should have refused. I shouldn't have wanted to do it.

We walk through the town center, which isn't all that big. Stella's office is in the town hall, but the greenhouses are a few blocks away.

"I'd like to be there all the time," she says. "Then I'd have everything in one place."

"Yes, that sounds better."

"But they want all the departments together. I know everything about garbage now, I share my office with waste disposal."

She continues her monologue about the organization of the town council. I find it difficult to concentrate on what she is saying, we have stopped in front of a gate and I look at the dense cypress hedges, they are dark, they look cool in spite of the heat, shady. The ground beneath them must be damp, I think of a poem by Christina Rossetti that appealed to me when I read her for my assignment, I can hear it in my head: "When I am dead, my dearest, / sing no sad songs for me; / plant thou no roses at my head, / nor shady cypress tree," there is a faint smell of resin, turpentine, an acrid smell, yet pleasant. Stella opens the gate and lets me in. There are three huge greenhouses behind the hedges, surrounded by flower beds and vegetable plots.

"Isn't it wonderful?"

Stella looks thrilled.

"Absolutely."

She opens the door of one of the greenhouses, I follow her inside. Even though it's warm outside the heat in the greenhouse is completely different, humid and sticky, it's hard to breathe at first. I can almost feel my hair beginning to curl. There is a damp smell and I can hear the faint sound of running water, I look around. In one corner of the greenhouse there is a little pond with mosaic lining the inside, different shades of blue, like Gabriel's ashtray, I think, like a little pool. Two big carp are swimming around in the pond, it is surrounded by rhododendron bushes, there are still a few flowers but they consist mostly of thick dark-green leaves, they look hard.

"You've got fish?"

Stella smiles.

"They've been here for a long, long time. This greenhouse goes back to the turn of the last century, that was when they made the fish pond, although at some point it had been covered over and built on, they found it when they were carrying out renovation work in the eighties. I'm sure those fish have been here since then, I think they can get pretty old."

I am breathing heavily from the heat, I can feel the dampness on my back. "God, it's hot."

"It's like South America. Peru, maybe. Look."

She points to a bench covered in orchids. It looks like a little forest, stalks poking up out of green moss, the flowers in every shade from white and pale pink to a wine-red so dark it is almost black. Their petals are velvety, some of them patterned with spots or blotches. There is a faint scent in the air, perfumed, sweet.

"That's my orchid collection," says Stella.

She looks proud, she leans toward one of the flowers, touches it gently.

"Nobody thought growing them in here would work," she says. "They're so sensitive. The temperature and humidity have to be perfect for them to flourish. We had a power outage last spring, I think it was in March when the temperature was still below freezing, we had a late spring last year. The power was only off for about half an hour, so they nearly all survived, but they reacted immediately. I've sorted out an emergency generator that kicks in if we have a power outage now, I don't know why there wasn't one here already. Although they used to grow mainly pansies and pelargoniums before. And heather, rows and rows of heather for those pizzeria containers . . . Heather can cope with most things."

I nod, although I know nothing about heather. I gently press the green moss surrounding the orchids with my forefinger, it is damp, springy. I try to remember when I last felt moss.

"But what are they for?" I say. "They can't go in the containers around the town, surely?"

"No, these are mine. I bought them with my own money, I'm just borrowing a little bit of space for them in here. But I'm sure I can come up with something. They'd make a good present when somebody on the council has a birthday, or retires or something."

She sets off again, I follow, past pots of small palms along one wall, Stella says they will stand in the square outside the town hall next summer, then she glances at her watch.

"I'm going to be late for my meeting, I must dash. Are you coming?"

We stay together until we reach the pedestrian area in the town center. I don't know anybody who walks as fast as Stella when she's in a hurry, I have to break into a trot to keep up.

"Are you going home now?" she says.

"I don't know."

"Or do you want to come back with me later?"

"I don't know," I say again.

"I'm in a hurry."

"I'll come with you later."

She nods.

"I'll be leaving at quarter to five, see you then," she says quickly before cutting across the square toward the council offices.

I don't know what I'm going to do with myself for a whole afternoon all alone in town, I wander around aimlessly. First of all I go back to the café where Stella and I had lunch, but there's nowhere to sit. Families on holiday are eating ice cream with strawberries, decorated with little paper parasols, some of the people are speaking German. The center is concentrated around the town hall square, and I spend a few hours in the shopping mall beside it, a depressing concrete structure that looks as if it could be in just about any Swedish town. The same retail chains as everywhere else, the same messy summer sales. I try on a dress in a deserted H&M that is chilly from the air-conditioning, decide to buy it. I had only one dress with me and I've worn it virtually every day, washing it in the hand basin at night and pegging it out so that the sun has dried it by the time I get up. The new dress is shorter, made of a light, floral fabric, intertwining stems and leaves.

Then I find a small library on a side street, there is a sofa in the poetry section and I flop down, pulling out odd books and reading in a vaguely preoccupied

way until half past four, when I head back to the
council offices. Stella is already waiting outside even
though it's only twenty to.

She raises her eyebrows at me by way of a greeting.

"Did you finish early?" I say.

"No, we said quarter to," she says.

"Yes?"

"Yes?" she repeats.

"Is your watch fast?" I say.

I see the furrow appear between her eyebrows.

"Maybe your watch is slow?" she says.

I sigh.

"Okay, sorry if I'm late."

She shrugs her shoulders, I follow her across the
square to the car.

Stella's mood rapidly improves when we get home.
Gabriel compliments her on the skirt she is wearing,
and she does a little pirouette in the hallway, laughs,
doesn't get changed as she usually does after work. Instead she ties an apron around her waist and starts to
help him with dinner. He is peeling carrots, he grabs
hold of her as she walks past, tips her backwards and
kisses her quickly, she laughs again. Then she gets
a bottle of wine out of the refrigerator and opens it,
pours three glasses and puts one on the kitchen table
in front of me. Gabriel interrupts his peeling to raise

a glass to her. I sit and flick through an interior design magazine Stella subscribes to, I have to look away when she walks behind him and runs one hand along his arm. A quick caress, a gesture that is ordinary and tender at the same time, I feel a stabbing pain in my stomach.

There is condensation on the outside of my glass, my fingers get damp when I pick it up to take a sip even though I don't feel like drinking wine tonight. I stare at an article about swimming pools, it's full of beautiful photographs of spectacular houses. One of them has a pool with the shorter side made of glass, overlooking a steep cliff, way down below is the sea, hissing waves breaking on black, jagged rocks. If that glass wall shattered you would die, I think. I think about Gabriel's hand on the back of my neck in the car, the way he pulled me toward him just as he did with Stella a few moments ago, the same firm movement. What did I actually imagine? That he would stop liking her just because he had kissed me? Even though I can see how unreasonable that idea is, watching them cook together makes me feel ill, the fact that they obviously enjoy each other's company. There is something between them that far outweighs a kiss, I think, there is a history, plans for the future, shared confidences, an entire existence. I've never had that kind of thing with anyone, and I definitely don't have it with Peter. With him it's like a delayed teenage relationship, where nothing feels safe or se-cure for more than the moment, where everything is replaceable, open to renegotiation. A kiss doesn't count for much against what Stella and Gabriel have; it was just a mistake, anyone can make a mistake.

I can feel my cheeks burning at the realization of how childish I am, mixed with disappointment, it feels as if my temperature has suddenly shot up. Somehow I had thought that things would be differ-ent, in some small way at least, but nothing is differ-ent, Gabriel has barely looked at me, not in anything but a perfectly correct way, friendly yet distant, as if I were no more than the visiting relative I am.

I have to get up from my place at the kitchen table and go and sit on the sofa on the patio, with the kitchen out of sight. I can hear Stella laughing, I close the door carefully behind me. I have brought my glass and the magazine with me, the water in the pool is a chilly turquoise, I stare at it and try to calm my thoughts. What is the matter with me? Can you do such a thing if there's nothing the matter with you? Perhaps there's something wrong in my brain, like with murderers, psychopaths, a basic lack of empathy. Although it isn't empathy I lack, it's more that I have the ability to close things off, push them away, block my brain from grasp-ing the consequences of my actions, it's always been that way. I have always thought of it as an extension of my lively imagination, but perhaps it's something else, some kind of mental disorder, a fault. Something that ought to be treated: there are watertight bulkheads between the different parts of my brain, I think, where there should be no dividing walls at all.

Then I get angry, thinking that he ought to understand, he ought to realize he can't do something like that and then pretend it hasn't happened, but perhaps that's the way he works. Perhaps it's like a game to him. Nothing is a game to me, nothing ever has been. I take everything seriously, I always have. That's how you end up not being kissed until you're twenty, I think, not because that's what you want but because you just can't mobilize that final lack of control that is necessary, the ability to go with the flow and just let things happen. Stella and I are alike in that way, in our need for control. But she has a purposefulness and a self-confidence that I lack, and that more than compensate, so she gets what she wants anyway.

I take a big gulp of my wine and lean back on the sofa, trying to work out what I have instead, but I can't come up with anything. I'm like Stella, I think. But not quite as good.

Both Stella and Gabriel are still in a cheerful mood at dinner. Stella seems slightly tipsy and tells us about a man at the council whom she doesn't get along with, she and Gabriel analyze him together, laughing, I feel superfluous even though they both make polite attempts to draw me into the conversation.

Stella excuses herself after we've eaten, she's going for a shower, Gabriel excuses himself without giving a reason and follows her up the stairs, I hear her laughing again, telling him to stop doing something although it doesn't sound as if she wants him to stop at all. I stay on the veranda, trying not to listen for sounds that will give away what they're doing, but although of course it's impossible not to listen I don't hear a thing. I think I ought to do some work on my assignment but I'm a little drowsy from the wine, I'm not used to drinking every night. However, I go and fetch some books from the pile on my bedside table, I open the one with the most attractive cover and flick through it aimlessly, I take another sip of my wine.

"Hi there," says Gabriel as he steps out onto the patio a while later. "How's it going?"

He sounds cheerful but friendly, he's looking at me with an expression I can't place, I almost think he looks a little bit lost, as if he's not quite sure how to behave. Maybe he feels the same as I do, I think. Maybe he's not in control of the situation at all, maybe he doesn't know how to handle it any more than I do.

The thought makes my anger ebb away, replacing it with a kind of tenderness, I smile at him.

"I thought I might do some work, but it's not going too well."

He nods, sits down beside me on the sofa, and reaches for one of the books, he leafs through it without appearing to take any notice of what it says, sighs, puts it down again.

"I guess it's not going too well for either of us," he says.

I look at him, at first I think he means the kiss and it's an invitation to talk about it, then I realize he means his writing. He reaches for his glass of wine, his arm brushes against mine, he's sitting very close to me. Suddenly all I want is to lean my head against his shoulder, to feel him pull me close and hold me tight. I am aware of his smell, it's faint but unmistakable once I have picked it up, he smells clean with a slight hint of smoke and then a soft scent of something sweet, like vanilla. I look at his arm where his T-shirt ends and his skin begins, I feel a tremendous desire to reach out and touch him, gently run my fingertips along his arm, along the veins just visible on the inside, it looks so soft.

"Everything will be fine," I hear myself saying. "I think you're making too much of an issue of this novel. You should just write."

He gives me a wan smile, I feel slightly stupid for saying anything at all, I have no idea what I'm talking about, no doubt he realizes that too.

I clear my throat.

"What I mean is, your writing always turns out well. You should trust in that."

"Kind of you to say so."

"I didn't say it to be kind."

There is a vase of sweet peas on the table now, spreading a perfume that seems to grow more intense as the day goes on. They clamber up a length of chicken wire in the kitchen garden, getting entangled in one another and in the wire, winding their tendrils like lianas around everything they can reach, greedily, clinging on tightly, some are almost impossible to pull free when you're picking them, I look at Gabriel's arm again, his hands, his fingers, imagining how it would feel if they touched me, if he reached out his hand and placed it on my leg right now, letting it find its way up my thigh, beneath the thin fabric of my dress. The scent of the sweet peas mingles with the vanilla coming from him, I quickly close my eyes and take a deep breath, it's a soft scent, powdery, it seems almost improbable that it can simply appear like this, it ought to be possible to extract it from the air somehow, concentrate it, bottle it.

Gabriel looks at me but says nothing, it is quiet now, no music tonight, just the singing of the crickets, his eyes are darting all over the place.

"Perhaps it's best if we go to bed now," he says quietly.

"Is that what you think?"

There is a tortured expression on his face now, I recognize it, it's the same look he had in the car, after he had kissed me, suddenly I realize he might be thinking exactly the same thing as me, perhaps he's finding this just as difficult as I am.

He nods, gets up slowly from the sofa.

"Yes," he says. "That is what I think, unfortunately."

I am woken by the noise of the vacuum cleaner, Gabriel is up early and doing the housework. He nods to me from the living room, where he is vacuuming the old Oriental rug that covers almost the entire floor.

I get myself some breakfast, make a sandwich, put the coffee on. When I open the cupboard door under the sink where the trash bag is kept, a cloud of tiny flies swirls out and a heavy, sweet stench hits my nostrils. This is the time of year they call the dog days, and with the unusual heat as well, everything goes bad straightaway. Stella mentioned it at dinner last night, the fact that it's barely possible to harvest anything because it's ruined almost immediately, they'd been talking about it on the news, weary farmers in Skåne with rotting vegetable crops. I wave my hand in the air to disperse the swarm of flies, then I hold my breath and tie the bag tightly before placing it in the doorway between the living room and the patio so that I won't forget to throw it out.

I eat my breakfast on the patio, I open Gabriel's book and begin to read. It's exciting from the very first page, creepily unpleasant, I think how strange it is that I don't remember it more clearly. One of the chapters ends with a short sex scene between the principal male character and a younger woman, I read it several times, feeling my cheeks burn.

Gabriel comes out onto the patio after a while, he looks hot, his thick hair is tousled. He shakes his head.

"That will have to do," he says to me, as if he wants me to agree with him, so I do.

"I'm sure it will."

"It's crazy, cleaning in this weather."

Then he notices what I'm reading, he reaches for the book, regards it with a critical expression.

"It hasn't aged very well, has it?" he says, looking at me.

"I was just thinking it was better than I remembered."

"Stella hates it."

I can tell from the tone of his voice that he isn't joking, there's the tiniest hint of bitterness there, and disappointment, a disappointment that has become a habit.

"Of course she doesn't," I say anyway, and he nods.

"She does. She hates the main character. I think she hates the story too, she hasn't said so, but that's what I think. Sometimes I don't know . . ."

He falls silent, looking at me with a searching expression.

"What?"

"Sometimes I don't know what I'm supposed to do to make her happy," he says, more quietly.

"She doesn't always show her appreciation very clearly," I say, also more quietly, as if I am afraid Stella might hear, although she isn't even home. "She never has."

He clears his throat.

"The cover is good anyway," he says cheerfully, drumming his fingers on the woman on the front.

"Absolutely."

"Do you know the story of this painting?"

"No."

"Her name was Elizabeth. She was married to Rossetti," he says, placing the tip of his forefinger on the drowned woman's chest. "And she sat for Millais. Or *lay*, to be more precise . . . in a bath full of cold water, looking as if she'd drowned, for several weeks. She got sick after that, she got pneumonia and died."

You can almost see it in her face, I think as I gaze at the cover, it looks gruesome. Her mouth is open, and her eyes, open but motionless, her face looks paralyzed as if it has stiffened in a moment of panic, as if she screamed out loud at the moment she realized she was actually in the process of dying. A penetrating scream, I think, a scream that would frighten the birds in the nearby bushes, making them take off in terror in a surge of beating wings, making the slow worms wriggle beneath stones and ferns and the rabbits hide in their burrows.

"Rossetti went mad with grief," says Gabriel. "He decided never to write poetry again. Perhaps he thought he wouldn't be able to. He simply gave up. And then he buried everything he had ever written along with Elizabeth, placed it inside her coffin . . ."

He smiles briefly.

"And then he changed his mind . . . and dug up her grave one night."

"What?"

Gabriel nods, looking very pleased with himself.

"It was several months after the burial, but when they opened her coffin she was still just as beautiful as when she died, her skin just as white and smooth, and her hair . . . You know that hair can carry on growing after death? She was lying there completely surrounded by hair, it was kind of . . . everywhere, filling the whole coffin, spilling out when they removed the lid, tumbling over the sides."

I shake my head.

"That can't possibly be true," I say, looking inquiringly at him, but his expression is serious, he holds my gaze.

"Yes, it is. It's true."

"It's just a story," I mutter.

Gabriel says nothing, he looks at the plastic bag in the doorway.

"The trash smelled so disgusting," I say quietly. "Something's gone rotten in there."

It takes an entire morning to read the rest of Gabriel's manuscript. He has printed it out now, a thick bundle with text on both sides. The ending is missing, he still isn't happy enough with it to show me. Perhaps he's far too self-critical, I think, because the rest of the manuscript is good, I just can't understand why he's so dissatisfied with it. The story is set in a small town in the winter, the sense of desolation and the cold are so well captured that I almost feel frozen in spite of the fact that it's 80 degrees outside.

He is cutting the grass in front of the greenhouse when I go out into the garden. It is cooler today, but it still seems like hard work. He smiles when he catches sight of me, but with a little hesitation in his smile, a hint of anxiety. I suddenly realize that perhaps my opinion actually does matter to him. I had thought that he had let me read the manuscript as a favor to me, so that I would have something to do—the way you treat a student intern, finding a job they can't possibly mess up, but when I see the tense expression on his face I realize that he will take notice of what I say.

He switches off the lawn mower.

"So," he says with a smile that looks strained, "what's the verdict?"

"It's really good," I say. "I can't understand what you're worried about."

He smiles, raises his eyebrows as if he's wondering if I'm really telling the truth, I nod.

"Really good," I say again.

Suddenly he no longer seems to be listening. Instead I can see that his eyes are fixed on my fingers, my nails. I am wearing a darker polish now, a deep cerise, like the darkest of the trembling cosmos flowers in the garden, their petals look almost like nails. Stella's nails are short and unpainted, she can't have long nails, they break when she's working, they split and tear, dirt and soil get stuck underneath them, it's not practical, it's impossible. I meet his gaze, his eyes are always dark but now they look almost black, just as they did in the car. He takes a step toward me, pulls me decisively toward him, and kisses me. I think to myself that I knew he was going to do it. I knew it when I chose the color, I knew he would like it, it's verging on the vulgar, I was thinking of him while I was painting my nails, like a magic spell. Perhaps I have known even longer, ever since that first evening when he was standing in the kitchen, when he met my eyes and held them fast.

His kiss is equally hard this time, almost violent. When I push my hands under his T-shirt his breathing becomes louder, I gently run my nails down his back and his breathing turns into a muffled groan, it arouses me, I press myself against him. We are leaning against the end of the greenhouse, he takes hold of one hand and locks it in a tight grip against the glass wall above my head, kissing me at the same time. I am also breathing loudly now. He holds on to my wrist as he draws me into the greenhouse, placing me firmly against the potting bench with my back toward him. Then he is behind me, quickly pulling up my dress, pushing my panties to one side. I was ready for this and yet I wasn't, his hands clasping my hips and then one hand between my thighs, he is breathing heavily, pushing himself against me, thrusting inside me as far as he can.

It's Saturday, Stella isn't working. Instead she is sorting out the plants in the greenhouse. There are palms growing in pots, a lemon tree and another angel's trumpet, much bigger than the one on the balcony, several feet high, a proper little tree in a big clay pot. I stand beneath it looking up at the heavy bell-shaped flowers, the sunlight filtering through the leaves and making them appear greenish-yellow as if they were filled with chlorophyll, glimpses of the sky between the leaves like flickering blue jigsaw puzzle pieces. I reach out and touch one of the bells. It is so big that it looks artificial, something about it seems almost menacing, the opening is like a mouth. I gently stroke it with my fingertips, it is as fine as a butterfly's wing but still feels strong, like parchment.

"That's poisonous," Stella says.

She is sowing seeds in a small propagator, meticulously making holes with a stick and carefully dropping a seed into each one.

"The flower?" I say.

"The whole plant. Every part of it is poisonous."

I quickly withdraw my hand.

There is a white wrought-iron chair next to the potting bench, I sit down on it, the image of me leaning over the bench shimmers before my eyes, Gabriel behind me, the grip of his hands on my hips, I think about the way he was breathing, the way he felt inside me.

"We ought to do something," Stella says suddenly.

The sound of her voice makes me jump.

"What?"

"Do something. Anything. Go somewhere, maybe."

"Yes, sure. Where?"

"Into town? To the sea? I don't know. Go and visit something, maybe. The palace?"

She looks at me with a challenging expression. I have to decide.

"Okay, let's go and visit the palace," I say.

As usual it's impossible to tell what she thinks of my choice, her face is blank, but at least she seems full of energy as she brushes off the soil and heads across the lawn.

"Marina wants to visit the palace," she says to Gabriel when we meet him on the patio, as if it was my idea. "You don't need the car this afternoon, do you?"

It's more of a statement than a question. He doesn't need the car, he's going to work. He takes a cup of coffee and disappears up the stairs.

Stella is a good driver under normal circumstances, but today she seems distracted. I notice that she forgets her turn signal at an intersection, and when she parks she is so close to the car next to her at first that I hold my breath and wait for the bang, nervously fingering my seat belt. But it's fine, she seems completely unmoved when she gets out of the car.

"I haven't been here for such a long time," she says, twirling the keys around her forefinger.

"How long?"

She thinks it over.

"I haven't been here since just after I moved in with Gabriel. We came one of the first weekends. It was fall then, it was so beautiful, all the different colors of the trees along the avenues. I thought it was so lovely, I remember thinking we should come here often. But we haven't been here once since then."

I nod.

"You'll have to come and stay with us again in the fall, then we'll come here so that you can see. You can have coffee and cake by the open fire. And you can pick chestnuts."

I smile, she looks at me and smiles back. We used to pick chestnuts when we were little, bucketfuls of them. I remember very clearly the feeling of breaking open the prickly green shell, how it opened up along the seams in a way that seemed too good to be natural. And the inside, spongy and white around the dark chestnut. It always felt cold in your hand at first, it was nice to squeeze in your palm, smooth and shiny, and there was that smell of fall, sweet and earthy, like something beginning to decay. Stella seems to have thought exactly the same.

"I was always so disappointed when they grew dull after a while," she says.

"Me too."

"One year I decided to save a whole bag of chestnuts, I put them in a shoe box under my bed. When I got them out they were all dull and shriveled."

"I did that too. I tried for several years in a row."

"Yes."

"I think I wondered whether you could varnish them to keep them shiny."

"Me too."

We laugh. The gravel path crunches beneath our feet, we're wearing almost identical shoes today, espadrilles, just different colors.

The palace dates from the beginning of the eighteenth century, it is white with two wings. An author used to live here, Stella says, but she's forgotten who it was. I tell her it doesn't matter. We sit down on a bench, there is a park behind the palace. You can see water a short distance away and you can tell from the air that it's the sea, the open sea rather than a lake, you can smell it, and you can hear it, there are gulls screaming far away, forming a backdrop of noise.

Stella clears her throat.

"I'm pregnant," she says.

She is looking at me steadily. I have to lower my eyes, I can't hold her gaze, the sound of the gulls seems so close now.

"What did you say?"

"I'm pregnant."

The smell of salt is coming off the sea and something else as well, something musty, almost nauseating, perhaps it's seaweed that has been washed ashore and is drying in the sun, glued to a rock.

"Congratulations," I hear myself say. "That's fantastic."

It sounds as hollow as I feel, but Stella doesn't appear to notice.

"You mustn't tell Gabriel. It's still very early and . . . well, I haven't told him yet."

"I promise."

I give her a hug, she throws her arms around me.

"We've been trying for such a long time. Ever since I moved here, virtually. He thought there was something wrong, but it's just taken a while, it's perfectly normal," she says, her face half buried in my hair.

"I didn't know . . ." I say. "I didn't know you were trying."

"I'd like to wait a little while, I've got so much going on at work right now. But Gabriel really wants a baby. He . . ."

She lowers her eyes.

"What?"

"He's almost become obsessed by it. He's not feeling too good at the moment, all this business with his book . . . There seems to be no end to it and he's never satisfied with it. And . . . he's getting older, of course."

I nod.

"I suppose it's only natural," she goes on. "But . . . I've had two miscarriages."

"What?"

"Very early on, I mean it's not uncommon . . . but he got so angry."

"He got angry with you?"

"Not with me, maybe. But angry. Furious, almost."

"Stella . . ." I begin without any idea of how I'm going to finish the sentence, I want to say something kind, that it's not her fault, even though I know that she knows that and it sounds childish, but it's the only thing I can come up with.

"It's not your fault."

Suddenly she has tears in her eyes.

"But what if it is?" she says quietly. "What if there's something wrong with me, and it will never work out? There's nothing wrong with Gabriel anyway, because I do get pregnant . . . it just doesn't seem to want to stay inside me, somehow."

She is crying now.

"Stella . . ." I say again, pulling her close, she weeps against my shoulder and I pat her hair, I feel awkward, I ought to say something wise and comforting but I don't know what. It feels as if the situation is upside down: the fact that I am consoling her when she has always taken care of herself, and then I think it isn't like that at all, because she has never consoled me, I have never wept on her shoulder. She shows that she cares by making demands on me instead, I think, she believes it's as easy for everyone else as it is for her, you just make a decision and get things done: science options in school, part-time work in a market garden, disciplined academic studies with no dropped points or missed assessments, boyfriend with a permanent job and a place of his own. This business with Gabriel is the first illogical thing she has done, the first thing that doesn't seem to have been part of a plan that was as straight as an arrow. And at the same time she entered into this illogical relationship with the same purposefulness she applies to everything else, convinced that it will work: a relationship with a considerably older man, the new job, the move to Skåne, the garden she has made exactly as she wants it. She has been talking about renovating the house too, doing up the kitchen and the bathroom, redoing the tiling, replacing the floors. Gabriel has opted out of the discussion, he's too comfortable, I should think it probably annoys him.

I stroke Stella's hair and she stops crying after a little while, she seems almost ashamed at having behaved with such a lack of control, and in public too.

She glances around to check if anyone is looking at us, digs a handkerchief out of her purse and blows her nose, tidies her hair.

"Do I look terrible?"

"No, of course not."

She gives a wan smile.

"I really want to wait before I talk to Gabriel about this. So don't say anything to him. About any of it."

"No, I promise," I say again.

Peter rings in the evening, his voice loud and clear over the telephone even though he's so far away, in Barcelona for the time being, they're going to carry on along the coast, perhaps go down to Gibraltar. He sounds happy but slightly awkward, I can hear voices in the background, some of them female, the sound of high heels on a tiled floor, a woman laughing, he says he's in a restaurant.

"Are you having a good time?" I ask.

"Absolutely. You'd like Barcelona."

"I'm sure I would."

I don't know what to say to him. The realization that it has only been a few weeks since we last saw each other but he has almost disappeared from my mind already is liberating. I don't even miss him when I hear his voice, I think, I don't care who that laugh belongs to.

"So how are things with you?" he says in that new, polite tone of voice.

"Fine. I'm not doing much, really. Reading and eating, mostly."

"Sounds good. Like a real summer holiday."

The thoughtfulness in his voice doesn't sound genuine to me, the fact that he's trying to pretend just makes me feel uncomfortable, I don't want to pretend any longer, and I don't want to talk to him anymore, I clear my throat.

"Listen, Stella's just shouted to me, she wants some help with dinner. So . . . you take care."

"You too."

We hang up at exactly the same time, very quickly, both equally relieved, perhaps.

———

Stella and I walk through the forest on our way down to the lake, over shiny tree roots and last year's fallen leaves. The trees around us are tall, it's like walking in a great hall of trunks, a cathedral with a ceiling made of treetops. I look up at the sky, blue flickering among the green, I see a bird way up high, sitting motionless on a branch and watching us. It is hot even in the shade beneath the trees, the air seems to be standing still.

By the side of the path there are mats of glowing green sorrel, I break off a few leaves and push them in my mouth. The taste is sour, just as I remember from the forest where we played when we were little, but I find it difficult to swallow the leaves when they grow soft in my mouth, I spit them out. Stella looks at me, her expression amused.

"You can use them in salads," she says.

I wrinkle my nose, she smiles.

The water in the lake is still and dark. Stella doesn't want to swim by the little sandy beach, but by some rocks a little farther on, it's nicer getting in there, you avoid that feeling that the ground is giving way beneath your feet. She has wound up her hair in a shiny knot on top of her head, and in her strapless swimsuit she looks like a film star, timeless, elegant. I feel clumsy beside her but I forget that as soon as the water envelops me, it feels fresher today, it's warm enough to be pleasant from the start, but yet it's cooling, I lie on my back, close my eyes, the surface of the water is almost body temperature. I feel so drowsy I'm afraid of nodding off, I can feel my head sinking farther beneath the surface the more I relax, the sounds around me become muted, slow. The water is the same color as syrup, or resin, I run my finger across the surface, it looks almost viscous, as if it has thickened, is in the process of setting. If the temperature were to drop suddenly Stella and I would end up like insects caught in a piece of amber, I think, like the people in Pompeii, trapped inside the syrup-colored frozen water of the lake instead of ash. The archaeologists could hack us out of the yellow ice one day, study us, the thought makes me smile.

A short distance away Stella's head is bobbing up and down, she swims out to the middle of the lake, turns and swims back, repeats this several times, I lose count of her lengths. Her strokes look slightly awkward, as if she is not entirely comfortable with them, but her expression is determined. Suddenly she is beside me, treading water, breathing heavily.

"This is fantastic exercise," she says between breaths. "You really do use your entire body."

I nod. Her movements produce small eddies of cooler water around us, I feel the gooseflesh on my arms, then a few seconds later they are smooth again as the blazing sun quickly warms up this new water too. Stella gazes over toward the shore on the far side of the lake, screws up her eyes, and points.

"Have you seen them?" she says. "I told you the water lilies would be flowering now."

I turn my head and there they are, a host of water lilies, like a floral cover on the surface of the water, it seems almost unbelievable that I didn't see them when I was here on my own. They move gently, even though the water looks completely still, perhaps there are currents down below tugging at their stems, they look indolent, majestic, like torches that have been slowly brought to the surface, up toward the light, blooming quietly and with dignity among the green pattern of their leaves.

"Can you pick them?" I say. "Take them home and put them in a vase?"

"Not in a vase, maybe. But it ought to be possible to put them in a bowl of water. Shall I go and get one?"

It's a long way to swim to the other side, perhaps she's overestimating her ability. I shake my head.

"I find them slightly revolting."

Stella laughs, pushes back a strand of hair that has escaped from the knot and fallen down over one eyebrow. Then she turns and swims back toward the rocks. A short distance out there is a large rock hidden just beneath the surface, the water swirling around it as a kind of warning. Stella heaves herself up onto it, waves to me, it looks weird, as if she's actually sitting on the water. I laugh, wave back, swim toward her.

"You look like the little mermaid," I say.

She laughs too, slips back into the water, we swim back to the shore together.

When we have dried ourselves with our faded towels we spread them on the rocks and sit down side by side. The stone is smooth and pleasant, like in the archipelago. I fiddle vaguely with some alder cones, Stella drinks water directly from an old juice bottle she has brought with her, swallowing great big gulps, then she takes a deep breath.

"I think I'm going to start swimming in the fall," she says. "In the mornings, before I go to work. The pool is right next door. I'd like to be a really good swimmer. And it makes you strong."

I steal a glance at her body. She is smaller and daintier than I am, I've always envied her that. She doesn't look as if she needs to take up swimming to keep in shape, and there is no sign of a rounded tummy yet. I spot a mark on her inner thigh, just below the edge of her swimsuit. It's a round mark, about the size of a shirt button or a small coin, dark against her smooth, pale skin, a livid dark red, almost purple. When she notices that I have seen it she quickly covers it with her hand, looks up at me, I think she looks as if she has been caught out, slightly embarrassed.

"What's that?" I ask.

She shakes her head, smiles anxiously.

"I'm so clumsy, I burned myself," she says.

"On what?"

"I dropped a cigarette."

She's nowhere near as good at lying as I am, and the thought that I am better than her at something is quite satisfying. There is something different about her tone of voice, something strained, besides which it's a poor explanation. It could easily be a burn, but a dropped cigarette would never make such a perfect round mark. And she would have had to have been smoking dressed in only her underwear. I give a little smile, she looks at me with an unconvincingly re-laxed expression.

"But you don't smoke, do you?" I say.

She looks away.

"Sometimes. At parties."

I drop the subject because it is obviously upsetting her. It amuses me slightly to have hit upon a sore point, even if I find it difficult to understand why. Perhaps there's something she finds embarrassing behind it, but dropping a cigarette on your leg is hardly some-thing to be so embarrassed about. But then it occurs to me that she might have done it on purpose, that she might have burned herself. I've only read about that kind of thing in magazines, and at first the idea seems alien, but the more I think about it, the more logical it seems. Stella, who is such a controlled person, always so conscientious—isn't that the kind of woman who does those things, is she punishing herself for some reason? I swallow, afraid of where my thoughts are heading: Stella weeping in my arms in the palace park, her "What if it's my fault," perhaps it's only a short step from there to punishing herself in a purely practical way.

I suddenly feel ill, I glance at Stella, who seems perfectly calm now, perfectly happy in the sun on the warm rocks. She passes me the bottle of water, rolls over onto her stomach, closes her eyes.

When Stella is at work and Gabriel has gone into town I go up the stairs, up to the first floor, into the bedroom. I don't know what I'm looking for, but I haven't been able to get the mark on Stella's thigh out of my mind. I want proof, one way or the other. At the same time I am trying to persuade myself not to make too big a deal of it, to take it easy—even this kind of thing could be a one-off, I think, a really bad day, I don't have any problems imagining that, even if I could never do something like that myself, but then Stella and I are different in that way too: her anger has always been more explosive, found more dramatic ways of expressing itself than mine. Perhaps she did it out of sheer defiance, a kind of regression to her teenage years, perhaps she regrets it with hindsight, thinks she overreacted and is embarrassed, perhaps that's why she doesn't want to talk about it.

Stella has kept a diary for as long as I can remember. I used to envy her the discipline she had even as a child: she really did write something every single day, even if it was only a brief entry. When we were little I used to be allowed to see what she'd written sometimes, then it all got more and more secretive and she started to hide her diaries, even though I would never have tried to find them and read them. I think it's unpleasant, knowing too much about other people, I've never understood that particular urge. I've always been surprised at the shameless curiosity of others: my friends rummaging in the drawers of my desk when they were left alone in my room when I was younger, or my first landlord in Stockholm who rented me a small, furnished one-room apartment full of stuff, and almost seemed to expect that I would go through drawers and photo albums, bundles of papers and videotapes.

There is no problem finding Stella's diary now, it's in the drawer of her bedside table along with a few bits and pieces: lip salve, some pens, tissues, and a packet of condoms, which makes me feel uncomfortable about my snooping, but I take out the diary anyway. It's covered in a shiny, Asian fabric with a pattern of blossoming fruit trees and birds against a pale-blue background, the same kind of notebook Stella used to have when she was little. I open the first page, it is dated just about twelve months ago, August last year, it must have been immediately after Stella and Gabriel came back from their holiday in Italy. All the entries are short, in Stella's neat and clearly legible handwriting: *Planning meeting with parks committee, decided to get rid of hyacinths outside town hall. Out for a meal with G after work* is the first entry. *Ordered bulbs, lots of yellow + broom for Slottsgatan and the square. Spoke to Sara, we might go there for the weekend in a few weeks.* It goes on in the same way: mostly notes about work, and a few details about what has happened at home, but in the same matter-of-fact tone. *G and I went to IKEA, bought shelves for the bedroom and storeroom. Sore throat, hope I don't get a cold before the conference next week.*

I put the book back in the drawer, surprised at the impersonal tone. Perhaps she no longer feels the same need for a diary, I think, perhaps she makes those notes about her everyday life because of some inherent sense of obligation. I close the drawer, smooth down the bedspread.

Gabriel barbecues in the evening, catfish, he shows it to me triumphantly before putting it on the grill. Ever since I arrived he has been saying that he ought to cook catfish because I've never had it, Stella makes potato salad with her own potatoes and radishes and red onions and herbs, she is proud of the fact that she grows so much herself. "If war breaks out we'll be self-sufficient," she often says, even if that isn't strictly true. I can hear her through the living room as she clatters about in the kitchen, muttering about blackfly on the dill, I hear Gabriel speak to her as he comes in to fetch something and they laugh together, a muted laughter that sounds intimate.

I am leafing through an old art book I found in one of the bookcases in the living room, its cardboard cover is yellowed and its color pictures of early Renaissance paintings are dull and faded, Italian frescoes with a somewhat tentative perspective. I wonder if the colors in the book were once sharper, if they were vivid red and blue when it was first printed, or if they have always looked like this, if it wasn't possible to print brighter colors at that time.

Gabriel makes a big thing of the fish when we're eating, it does look beautiful, patterned with lines from the grill, and it tastes good, although I don't think it's anything special.

"What do you think?" he says when I've taken the first bite.

"Delicious," I say.

"Try it with a little squeeze of lemon."

He passes me a dish of lemon wedges, I squeeze a few drops of juice over my piece of fish, taste again, nod to him. Then I empty my wineglass, gulping it down. It's good wine, easy to drink. I reach for the bottle and top up my glass, Stella is talking about some occasion when Gabriel made a complete mess of his catfish and they both laugh, I'm not listening. We have a secret, I think, a secret is a confidence and confidences mean something, they bind people together. This guilt is like a tie, I think. We have exchanged guilt as others exchange rings. We carry it together now, the knowledge of a betrayal.

He is still not looking at me, he is looking at Stella, he seems particularly attentive to what she says, laughing when she tells him about something that was in the paper, they have so much fun with the local paper that makes news out of nothing, particularly during the summer when nothing happens; articles about people showing off their enormous record-breaking vegetables and amusingly shaped potatoes, a story with a happy ending about a hamster that disappeared then returned to its owner, they laugh together. The feeling in my stomach is new, it is jealousy and something more, it feels like nausea, like a distant childhood memory of having fallen and gotten the wind knocked out of me so that at first I can't get any air, I am breathing but nothing happens, perhaps something inside me has locked in some kind of cramp, the nausea washes over me when he looks at Stella with his most loving expression, full of tenderness, he's never looked at me that way. He has looked at me in other ways, dark, aroused, it's not enough, when I see how he looks at Stella I know it's not enough for me, not anymore. Look at me, I think, look at me with that loving expression, look at me and stop laughing. But he doesn't stop.

The living room is like a jewelry box, I think as I stand on the thick Oriental rug, it is dark red, its pattern like prisms, diamonds, and the crystal chandelier on the ceiling glitters like an old lady wearing row upon row of necklaces. And then there are the books, shelf upon shelf, the pictures, the squashed-down sofa, the tiled stove, a bank of pelargoniums, I would be envious of anybody who got to live in a house with a room like this, does she appreciate it? Maybe she thinks it's too cluttered, that it attracts the dust. She hasn't said much about the house apart from the odd comment about things that don't work, and then that business of wanting to renovate the kitchen and bathroom, maybe she really wants to live somewhere else, preferably in Stockholm of course, or maybe in Malmö, just spending the summer here, and perhaps the odd weekend during the rest of the year.

I run my fingers over a row of book spines, wondering whether I ought to read one of them. On a stool there is a pile of Stella's books, books about flora and gardens, I pick one up, it is older than the rest. *The Countryman's Reference Book, compiled with the assistance of numerous specialists*, it is heavy, bound in dark-brown leather with the title in gold on the front. I flick through it from the back: threshing, thistles, sowing, root vegetables, rhubarb, pears, parasites, I stop, glance at the illustrations. They are disgusting yet fascinating, making me think of the clumps of blackfly on the nasturtiums, I skim through the text: *Parasite: refers to a plant or animal that acquires its nutrition from another living organism, which is then referred to as the host plant or host animal. Holoparasites occur in only a few cases among the higher plants in Sweden. As a rule they cause damage to the host by depriving it of nutrition, producing unhealthy growths, or destroying the tissues which have been attacked, thus leading to sickness and death,* the room is stuffy, we ought to open the windows more, but perhaps it wouldn't make any difference on days like this, or in summers like this, with its sticky, motionless air, we could have all the windows and doors wide open and it still wouldn't be any cooler or fresher.

Suddenly Gabriel is standing in the doorway, I close the book.

"What are you doing?"

"I thought I might try and find something to read."

He nods, walks over to one of the bookcases and seems to be looking for a particular book, I am aware of his smell, I close my eyes briefly and think of the greenhouse, his kisses, his grip on my arms, I can feel my cheeks begin to burn immediately.

"Here."

He passes me a small, thick book bound in blue leather. *Selections from the Poetical Works of Algernon*

Charles Swinburne, it says on the cover. The pages are fragile and yellowed, their edges uneven. Someone must have used a blunt knife to slit them open.

"I think you'd like it. And it fits in well with your assignment."

"Do you like it?"

He clears his throat.

"It's hard to find anything more elegant than this," he says. "And at the same time it's also hard to find anything more pathetic. Do you understand?"

His expression is different now, softer, his voice too, and at last he is looking at me in the way I want him to look at me. I nod, thinking that this is the way I want it to be, I want him to take out more books, hand them to me, look at me with that kind expression, wanting me to understand. I think that I really do want to understand.

I hear him talking on the telephone in the kitchen. He is leaning over the draining board, doodling absentmindedly on the notepad he and Stella usually use for the shopping lists. He can't see me, but I can gaze at him from behind, his shoulders, his arms where the sleeves of his T-shirt end. The fingers of one hand are drumming impatiently on the draining board, I realize he's waiting for something on the phone. Then he clears his throat.

"Yes, I called earlier," he says. "It's about the insurance."

He is silent for a moment, listening.

"But I've already keyed in the fucking client number," he says in a tone that is both irritated and weary. "Surely that's why they've put me through to you?"

He sighs, leafs through a bundle of papers in front of him and begins to read out a long sequence of numbers.

"No, four, seven. *Four, seven.*"

He runs a hand through his hair, it's something I've seen him do many times now, it seems to be a reflex action. I like to see him do it, no doubt he's done it all his life, he probably started when he was a teenager and has done it ever since, not so much out of vanity these days as out of habit. He has said that the car insurance policy guarantees that someone will come and pick up the car if there's something wrong with it, he's already called several times but no one has come.

He sighs again.

"What do you mean, they couldn't find us?"

He listens, puts down the pen he is holding in his hand.

"But why didn't you call then? No, I realize that. But the person who was supposed to be picking up the car, why didn't he call? Or she? Why didn't someone ring?"

He picks up the pen again.

"Are you completely fucking incompetent? Do you want me to send you a street map?"

He listens, making a few unsuccessful attempts to interrupt the person on the other end, mumbles "yes" now and again before saying in a quiet and controlled voice: "Right. Thank you very much."

There is a faint beep as he presses the button to end the call, he hurls the telephone down on the draining board.

"For fuck's sake!" he yells. *"Fucking idiots!"*

He almost spits out the last two words, I hear the phone slide into the sink, landing with a rattling noise. He disappears from my field of vision.

"Fucking idiots!" he yells again, then I hear a bang, the sound of something breaking, plastic cracking, scattering all over the kitchen. A little button with a "5" on it bounces out into the hallway and lands almost at my feet, I quickly back away, quietly parting the bamboo curtain in the doorway, slinking into the little porch with its potted plants and out onto the lawn, leaving Gabriel and his anger in the kitchen.

When Stella gets home from work it's still only early afternoon, there isn't much for her to do in the middle of summer. I am sitting reading on the sofa on the patio. It's the hottest day so far, they were talking about it on the radio, record temperatures in several places around the country. The weather is all they talk about on the news, it's the hottest summer since records began sometime around the beginning of the twentieth century. A few clouds are building up on the horizon, but the sun is still shining mercilessly.

"Do you think we're going to have a thunderstorm at last?" says Stella, squinting up at the clouds.

I shake my head.

"They didn't mention anything about a storm."

I am finding it difficult to concentrate on the book even though I think it seems good, I feel restless, I flick back and forth between the poems. A thunderstorm is what's needed, a discharge of electricity and a decent downpour. Stella sticks her finger into several plant pots with a troubled expression, she looks pale in her light dress, her forehead is shiny.

"How are you feeling?" I say.

She shrugs her shoulders. "Okay. I think I might take a walk."

"Do you want some company?"

She shakes her head.

"No, you carry on reading. Is Gabriel home?"

"He was going over to Anders's place to pick something up."

She nods. "What time is your train?"

"Around seven. Ten past, I think."

"We can have dinner before you go, can't we?"

"That would be good."

I can see her for a long time, I watch her cut across the lawn and head off toward the main road. She's probably going down to the lake, that's where she usually goes. I read a few more lines in my book, when I look up again she has disappeared.

Gabriel gets home a while later, muttering something about the fact that they haven't picked up the car yet. He hasn't mentioned either his outburst of rage or the broken telephone, he must think I didn't notice anything. I'm no good at dealing with anger, I'm not used to it.

"This is really good," I say, holding up the book as he passes me on the patio. He stops.

"That's great, I knew you'd like it."

I feel happy when he smiles at me.

"*There are sins it may be to discover, / There are deeds it may be to delight. / What new work wilt thou find for thy lover, / What new passions for daytime or night?*" I read, he laughs.

"That's cool. Is it 'Dolores'?"

"Yes."

"*I could hurt thee—but pain would delight thee.*"

He is looking straight at me as he speaks the line, I swallow.

"Is that what it says?"

He nods.

"I haven't gotten that far yet."

Behind him the air above the lawn is quivering with the heat, it looks like melted glass. There are hardly any insects in the air now, I realize I can't even hear any birds, perhaps they've moved into the forest, trying to find a cooler spot. It's as if the whole of nature is trembling before the heat, surrendering to it.

"Isn't Stella home yet?" says Gabriel.

"Yes, she's gone for a walk."

He nods.

"Do you know where she went?"

"Down to the lake, I think."

Suddenly he is standing behind me, he places his hands on my shoulders and lets them slide down my bare arms, I close my eyes, I feel my skin turn to gooseflesh at his touch. He gathers up the hair at the back of my neck in a bunch, lifts it up and tugs at it experimentally, playfully at first, then harder, forcing my head back until I am looking straight up at the sky, flat and dark cobalt blue, he leans over me, gazes at me, *I could hurt thee—but pain would delight thee*, his eyes are dark now.

"You ought to come inside with me for a while," he says.

The back of my neck is hurting, and the roots of my hair, I try to nod even though it's impossible, but he seems to be able to tell, he quickly lets go of my hair, disappears through the door leading into the living room. I get up from the sofa and follow him.

Part Two

The train is on time today as well, but now the flat landscape is gray, there is mist in the air. The dampness makes my hair curl and it quickly finds its way under the collar of my coat, making me shiver even though it is probably not particularly cold.

Gabriel is late, there isn't a soul in sight at the station. I read the placards advertising the evening papers on the wall of the closed newsstand, the tips and puzzles in the magazines: holiday buffet menu, crochet patterns, free crossword pullout. When Gabriel finally arrives he seems to be totally unaware that he is late.

"Oh no, have you been waiting?" he says, sounding surprised.

"We did say twenty past."

"Sorry, I thought we said twenty to."

"It's fine."

He gives me a hug, pulling me close and holding me tight. I bury my face in his scarf and inhale his smell, it's the same smell as in the summer. It is sweet, almost too sweet, bordering on nauseating, but I like it, it makes me feel safe. It's as if it makes the world shrink to the small area around him pervaded by that smell. I don't want to let go of him. He is wearing a dark coat that looks new and expensive, it suits him. I tell him, he smiles and says I'm lovely.

We don't say anything in the car. The landscape is completely different now, the fields that were yellow last summer are black, torn up, they look wounded, as if someone has raked them with nails as long as talons. One field is flooded after all the rain we have had during the fall, it has turned into a small lake with two swans gliding around like glowing patches of white. It is almost impossible to make out a horizon, land and sky merge into a gray mist. It's warm in the car, foggy with condensation.

"How's your assignment going?" asks Gabriel.

"What?"

"Rossetti?"

"Oh . . . I've hardly done any work on it at all. What about your book?"

"It's finished."

I look at him.

"I finished it at the end of September."

"Right . . . and were your publishers happy with it?"

He gives a small smile.

"They love it. They're going to try to get it out pretty quickly, by the spring."

"Wow. Congratulations."

He nods absentmindedly, his index fingers drumming on the wheel as he increases the speed of the windshield wipers, the rain is coming down more heavily now.

This is not the colorful fall Stella talked about when we were at the palace, not the picture-postcard, crisp October fall with high, clear air and vivid colors she thought I should come back for, that fall has been and gone. This is late fall, raw and rainy. I can no longer smell the rotting leaves, it is no longer possible to tell that it was once summer. The entire landscape is in a state of torpor, it has resigned itself, let go. No fall colors, only brown and gray, no leaves left on the trees, they are lying on the ground now, sodden in the puddles, crushed, a mush of fallen leaves, covering the lawn. I know you're supposed to rake them up, even if I can't remember why. Is it because the grass can't get any air if you don't? Or light? I think the leaves can keep the grass warm this winter, perhaps it might be happy under there, nice and cozy beneath its blanket of leaves.

.The garden is in the process of decay. The sunflowers look like scarecrows now that they have gone over, their seed heads black and wet, their leaves straggling and shriveled. I pull on Stella's Wellington boots that are in the back porch and take a walk around the garden, noticing the tomatoes that ripened but were never picked, their split skins exposing the dried flesh, rhubarb with leaves as big as umbrellas, the stalks so thick they are presumably inedible. They taste best before they get too big, as far as I remember, then they become bitter, woody. The pods of the sugar snap peas are swollen and lumpy, distorted, also too big for anyone but the worms to eat. Only the parsley is still green, glowing amid all the brown and gray, tiny drops of water have collected in its curly leaves. I break off a piece and push it in my mouth, it has the harsh taste of iron. A few sparse marigolds are still flowering stoically in the borders.

In the greenhouse most of the plants are dead. Those that are still alive are overgrown, they should have been cut back or thinned out. Only the trees in pots appear to be thriving: the palms, the lemon tree, and the big angel's trumpet. I stick my index finger in the angel's trumpet pot, the soil is dry. It looks a bit droopy but healthy, Gabriel must have watered it. I fill the watering can underneath the potting bench and pour water into each pot until it overflows. As if I thought it might be possible to fix them in retrospect; it is a childish idea. But I don't stop pouring, I stare at the water flowing out of the holes in the bottom of the pots, running across the floor in little black rivulets, disappearing down the cracks between the paving stones.

"I'm thinking of moving away from here for a while," says Gabriel when we are sitting in the living room in the evening. He has made tea and sandwiches, lit a fire in the old tiled stove, and put a record on the stereo, it feels lovely, almost like the summer.

"Where will you go?" I say.

He shrugs his shoulders.

"I don't know yet. Abroad, maybe. I thought I could come back here in the summer, but right now I think I need to be somewhere else for a while."

"So . . . when are you moving?"

My voice sounds small. He doesn't appear to notice.

"As soon as I can. As soon as I find a place to live."

I feel the tears overwhelm me without any warning, all at once my eyes are burning and then I am weeping, sobbing violently, totally out of control, I can see the tears falling from my eyes and dripping onto my legs, which I have drawn up under me on the sofa, it looks like rain, almost unreal. My whole body shakes as I gasp for breath.

Gabriel looks at me in surprise.

"Hey . . ." he says, he sounds so kind, so calm, and suddenly I am in his arms and he is holding me, I cling on tight, I have no intention of letting go. He strokes my hair and I lay my head against his shoulder, my face against his neck, breathing in the smell of him and sobbing even harder because of it. He smells so warm, he is holding me properly now, his arms around my back, and he mumbles that of course I can come and visit him whenever I like. He is wearing a lamb's wool sweater and I push my hands up inside it, I would really like to crawl right underneath it, stay there. The shirt he has on is easy to undo, and he doesn't protest. He pulls off his sweater and I part his unbuttoned shirt and lay my cheek against his chest, curling up in his arms.

He reaches for a checked blanket lying on the arm of the sofa, spreads it over me, and I pull it over my head until I am in a kind of snug haven against his chest, I can hear his heart beating and it is warm under the blanket now, Gabriel's arms around me, his skin, his smell, his breathing, calm and even. Take care of me, I think, take care of me, I have stopped crying now, my body feels heavy and weary, I want to go to sleep, just like this, and I do.

⎯⎯⎯⎯⎯⎯⎯⎯

I wake up on the sofa with a stiff neck. Gabriel has fetched the duvet from the guest room and spread it over me along with the blanket, but I am still frozen. It is raining outside, a slow and monotonous November rain, dripping from the roof onto the window ledges.

Gabriel doesn't seem to be home. My head feels woolly, as if I had a hangover, but I didn't drink at all yesterday. It's the weeping, I can still feel it in my sinuses and behind my eyes, I press my eyebrows gently with my hands. The inside of my head feels tender, sore. I wind the duvet around me, go into the kitchen, and switch on the coffee machine. The floor is cold, I should have brought a pair of slippers. It's almost eleven o'clock in the morning but it isn't all that light outside, it's a uniform gray, a flat, nondescript light. Yesterday the automatic exterior lighting came on just after two o'clock in the afternoon. Anders and Karin in the house across the field have put Christmas lights in one of their trees, a spindly fruit tree completely enveloped in little sparkling lights, you can see it from the balcony. Gabriel showed it to me yesterday when we went for a walk around the house and he said everything is more or less the same here really, and the bedroom upstairs was big and empty and the floorboards creaked in a way I don't remember at all from the summer and I thought no, nothing is the same here. And the fruit tree was shining from across the field.

I pour my coffee into one of the blue-and-white cups. There is an unopened carton of milk in the refrigerator and I think that Gabriel must have bought it for me, he remembered I take milk in my coffee. He drinks his black. I flick through the newspaper on the kitchen table without reading a single article, the letters in the headlines seem to be moving around in front of my eyes. Perhaps I've cried so much I've damaged my eyes. Maybe protein from my tears has stuck to them, in lumps that will stay there forever and make me go blind eventually. I have to knock wood, I rub the thick surface of the kitchen table hard with my fingers, I blink rapidly several times. I am perfectly normal. There is nothing wrong with my eyes.

I see something moving outside the kitchen window, at first I think it's a branch but then I see it's Nils. I open the window and speak to him and he immediately runs to the front door, I can hear him meowing. When I let him in he rubs himself against my legs. He's wet, his entire coat is covered in little drops of water, he looks as if he is studded with diamonds. I tear off a sheet of paper towel and gently wipe his back, he looks at me in surprise.

He goes and lies down on the sofa in the living room, where it is still warm from my body, curling up on the blanket. I want to lie down beside him, I want to curl up too and stay under the duvet, but I have to start sorting out Stella's things, I can't stay here indefinitely. They've let me start the C-course in art history even though I haven't finished my assignment from last semester yet, they made an exception, special circumstances. I cried in the senior tutor's office, I have cried everywhere. I miss seminars these days, I have been given permission to take slightly more time off than is really allowed, but I have to promise to read, it's for my own good, I mustn't get too far behind because otherwise it will be difficult to catch up. My books are in the guest room, not even unpacked, I ought to make a start tonight, I won't get any more of my student loan if I don't achieve a certain number of points this semester, that's a horrible thought.

When I get upstairs I can see the apple tree sparkling across the field. Perhaps they've forgotten to switch the lights off, or else it's so dark outside that they come on automatically even though it's the middle of the day. The sky is gray, the color of lead, as if there were snow in the air, but the temperature is well above freezing and the only thing that comes is rain. The lawn felt spongy yesterday, sodden. It will turn into a bog if it carries on raining.

Stella's clothes are still hanging in the big closet in the bedroom. There's not a great deal, she didn't keep anything she had no use for, I quickly go through the closet: jeans, sweaters, a few winter coats, shoes, some dresses, the suits she used to wear when she had a meeting in the council offices, negotiating budgets, things she didn't really want to do. Gabriel has told me to take whatever I want and put the rest in bags so that he can give it away to charity, but I don't want to keep anything. Everything smells of Stella, it's as if the entire closet is impregnated with her cool perfume, I shove the clothes into plastic bags, I just want rid of them. The only thing I can't bring myself to push into a bag is her white angora cardigan. It hardly smells of anything, perhaps a faint hint of fabric conditioner with an apple scent, perhaps slightly musty, she probably hadn't worn it for a long time. I run my fingertips tentatively over the soft white wool, it's so beautiful, silky and fluffy, like stroking a pet. In front of the full-length mirror in the bedroom I pull off the sweater I am wearing and cautiously put on the cardigan instead, it feels lovely against my skin, I can understand why she liked it. I stretch, let down my hair, which I had gathered in a knot at the back of my neck, look at myself from different angles. We're a little bit alike, I think. Not so that you would get us mixed up. But in ways that are more difficult to pin down, something to do with posture, proportions.

On the balcony Gabriel's computer is switched on as usual, surrounded by piles of books and papers and the dolphin ashtray. I touch it gently, stroking its back, the brass feels cool against the palm of my hand. There is an art book underneath the ashtray, *Une étude sur la peinture symboliste* it says on the cover, a little bit of a yellow Post-it note is sticking out between two pages and I open the book there. A painting of a young woman covers almost the whole double spread, it is similar to the cover of Gabriel's novel but there are no flowers floating on the surface of the water in this picture, no bushes and no greenery surrounding her. I am not very good at French but I have no problem understanding this title: *Drowned*.

I quickly close the book, turn around, and give a start as I see myself in the full-length mirror. Not so that you would get us mixed up, but almost, I think as I feel my heart beating hard and fast, I find it difficult to get my breath as I fumble with the buttons of the cardigan, they are small and round and mother-of-pearl and my fingers can't get hold of them properly. When I have managed to undo the top two buttons I pull the cardigan over my head in something approaching a panic and throw it in a heap on the floor, it lies there like a quarry brought down, rendered harmless. I fold my arms over my chest to avoid seeing my body in the mirror, I stand there for a while trying to breathe deeply and calmly until my heart slows down and I am able to put on my own sweater with trembling hands.

It is quiet in the house now, it feels different from the summer, the sounds I hear are new. The house clicks and creaks and at night the wind blows and the rain hammers against the window ledges, loud and persistent, a branch scrapes against something, rasping and banging, dull and repetitive. I curl up under the duvet, making myself as small as possible. There are drafts everywhere, Gabriel says the place really needs renovating properly if it's going to be possible to live here all year round, it needs proper insulation. He mentioned it in the summer and I thought he was exaggerating, that it wasn't really a problem, you'd just need an extra blanket at night. But now I have an extra blanket at night, and I realize he was right.

He sleeps alone up there now, on one side of the big double bed in the room where the apple trees in the garden cast long shadows on the ceiling. Every time I picture him there, and wonder if he is sleeping or lying awake like me, I see myself beside him in the bed. Very close to him, just like on the sofa when I fell asleep with my head resting on his chest. And then I have to push the thought away at once, I am sick in the head, abnormal, disgusting, and then all the other thoughts come crowding in like a film rolling through my mind: they pulled her out of the lake, I have imagined it a hundred times, a thousand times, the serious faces of the people on the rocks by the lake, the police, Gabriel. I can see eels in her hair, it is a horrible picture and I try to keep it at bay, but it always comes back: the eels in the lake, around her face, among her curls down at the bottom. Sometimes I see her with eels instead of hair, writhing, slippery, thick, shiny sausages all over her head and down over her shoulders. I always imagine that her eyes were closed, that she looked as if she was sleeping. And that she looked as if she was sleeping when she was lying there on the bottom too, while the eels were building their nests in her hair. She was afraid of snakes, she would have been so frightened if she had woken up and realized what was happening.

Gabriel has started to go for long walks during the day, I see him crossing the misty fields: a black silhouette slowly moving along the gravel road, he stops, looking at something or lost in thought, he stands in the same spot for a long time, following a crow with his gaze. I am upstairs, still sorting out Stella's things, I have gone through the bathroom cabinets. "Take whatever you want," Gabriel said again, but I have thrown almost everything away. All that expensive makeup, the creams, the shampoo, little tablets of soap, bath oil, it's almost filled an entire bag. I have kept a bottle of Stella's perfume because I couldn't bring myself to drop it in the bag, and two small unopened boxes containing Dior nail polish, still sealed in plastic film. She must have bought them on some trip, duty free, I find it difficult to imagine her buying such expensive nail polish in an ordinary shop. I picture her standing at the perfume counter at the airport thinking she's on holiday now, maybe there's a chance for her nails to grow before she has to start digging again, she chooses two bottles almost at random, thinking that she will sit on the balcony of her hotel room in the evenings, drinking a glass of wine, watching the sun set over the water and painting her nails, which are finally showing above the tips of her fingers like tiny, rising half moons. Perhaps it was when they went to Italy, they were there last summer. Somewhere on the Amalfi coast, a small town with a pretty name, they sent me a postcard.

Stella didn't have many books or records, I keep a few of each: a couple of New Order albums, it was

Erik who listened to them originally, the records might even have belonged to him. Stella always adopted her boyfriends' taste in music in spite of the fact that she wasn't particularly interested in music herself, or maybe that was why. She had almost no fiction, instead I pick out some of her botanical books: all the volumes in the series *The Flora of Scandinavia* and Rousseau's *Letters on the Elements of Botany,* which I know she loved. I pack them in a box along with one or two other things that I find in her closet: school yearbooks, a shoe box full of photographs, an old jewelry box I know my grandmother gave her when she was little. It contains some necklaces in a tangled heap, tarnished silver, gold chains with pendants in the shape of hearts and four-leaf clovers, the kind of thing you get when you're christened or confirmed. I put pile after pile of magazines into another box, perhaps they can be given away. Old fashion magazines, interior design, gardening, several of them are foreign, with beautiful glossy covers featuring English gardens. There is a pile of old catalogs, page after page of seeds and perennials, shrubs and fruit trees. I drop them into the garbage bag along with the bathroom stuff.

"How's it going?"

Gabriel's voice makes me jump. He is standing in the doorway, he is wearing his outdoor shoes and his coat, his hair looks damp.

"It's hard work."

"Do you want some help?"

"No, it's okay. But thanks."

He smiles at me, nods.

"I'm going to do some shopping. Would you like to come with me? Or is there anything you want from the store?"

I shake my head.

"I'd really like to get this finished. But maybe you could get some fruit? Satsumas?"

He nods again.

"Do you remember where Stella bought these?"

I show him the little boxes containing the nail polish, he looks thoughtful.

"I bought them for her. When we were going to Italy. But she never used them."

"I might keep them."

"Actually, I think she said she was going to give them to you."

He gives me another little smile, then disappears down the stairs.

I watch him cut across the lawn to the car. He is using Stella's car these days, he still hasn't gotten the engine of his car fixed, it would be expensive. Hers is newer, small and silver-colored and almost silent when you're sitting in it, as if it's padded.

There are yet more gardening magazines on the

shelf of Stella's bedside table, I put them in the box with all the rest. The contents of the drawer are the same as back in the summer, I pick up the pale-blue shiny book, flick through it halfheartedly. *Arranged with M that she will come later in the summer* I read before closing it quickly. What do you do with a dead person's diary? I can't throw it away, all her thoughts and notes, it just feels so wrong. I leave it in the drawer, Gabriel can decide.

In the evening I paint my nails. I have opened the boxes, one bottle is a pearly pink and looks summery, the other is a deep, dark red, and that is the one I choose. Gabriel came back from town with several kilos of satsumas, the sharp kind I like best, and I have already lost count of how many I have eaten: five, six, maybe seven. One thumbnail is already stained yellow from peeling them, it looks the same as it did under the water in the lake in the summer, the disgusting yellow water. I brush the expensive nail polish decisively over my thumbnail and it covers perfectly, giving a beautiful, even finish. I am sitting on the bed in the guest room. I have hung Stella's white cardigan on a hanger on the outside of the closet, it hangs there like a little work of art, white on white with its mother-of-pearl buttons gleaming indolently. There are no flowers on the bedside table

now, nor in the window, the room is bare, the walls
are white and the floor covered in a white glaze. It feels
like a cell, the way I imagine it looks inside a convent.
There's a convent nearby, we drove past it in the summer, Gabriel pointed it out and said it was one of the
strictest orders. Once you step inside the high stone
walls surrounding the convent garden you never come
out, not even when you die. The nuns are buried in the
little churchyard that forms a part of the garden.

The nail polish dries quickly, becoming hard and
shiny. I used to have terrible nails, they were soft and
split and broke and were uneven. Now they grow
quickly and are strong, I don't know why. Perhaps
I'm eating better now. I drum them on the bedside
table, enjoying the rapping sound as I look around
the room. There ought to be something on the walls
in here: a picture, a painting, anything, these bare
walls are unpleasant. I think of one of Rossetti's paintings, the one depicting the annunciation. The walls
in that room look almost the same as these: white,
like a convent. Mary has crawled up onto the bed and
is cowering in one corner, she looks afraid, defensive,
the angel is offering her flowers, they are also white,
lilies.

Rossetti moved out into the country when he got
older. Perhaps it was a house like this one, with a big
garden and lots of flowers. He and Swinburne lived
there together, took care of each other, acquired

animals, exotic animals, although I don't know which ones. It doesn't matter, it's a good story. I imagine they had a giraffe in the garden, I can see it grazing the tops of their English apple trees.

I really ought to try to finish my assignment. Art history isn't as much fun as it was at the beginning, when we had long lectures in dimly lit rooms, with hour after hour of slides. I felt as if the rest of the world disappeared as I learned about the different orders of Greek columns, mosaics and frescoes, the archaic smile, I can almost lose myself now in the memory of it: the lecturer's pleasant voice and how old-fashioned it felt, the fact that someone was standing there tell-ing me about ancient Greece and all I had to do was listen and learn it all for the assessments, I got almost everything right in most of them. It's not as much fun now, there's so much theory. Suddenly the book on Gabriel's desk comes into my mind, the Post-it note on the page with the drowned woman. Perhaps he had thought of using the picture for the cover of his first novel. I try to remember if the book was there in the summer but it's impossible, the entire desk is covered in great piles of books and papers.

Suddenly he is standing in the doorway and I jump, he smiles at me.

"I seem to keep scaring you."

I give him a little smile.

"You have to stop creeping up on me like that."

"I'm not creeping up on you."

He catches sight of Stella's cardigan on the closet door, he goes over to it, runs his hand over the soft angora.

"Are you keeping it?" he asks.

"I don't know, it just felt wrong to shove it in a plastic bag."

He nods.

"You ought to wear it."

"Really?" I say dubiously.

"Yes. I think it would suit you."

It's an unpleasant thought after the panic I felt when I tried it on, and wouldn't it be a bit strange, I think, a dead person's clothes, what do you do with dead people's clothes? Shove them in garbage bags while you're still crying, give them away, do people ever regret it? There's something so intimate about clothes.

I make no comment, instead I hold out my hands to show Gabriel.

"Look."

He screws his eyes up slightly, doesn't seem to grasp at first what he's supposed to be looking at, but then he sees the bottle of nail polish on the bed and takes hold of my wrist, examines my fingers.

"Wow."

His grip is firm. I try to withdraw my hand but he holds on to it, looking into my eyes. I wouldn't be able to free myself even if I really tried, I think, and the thought excites me, I have to look away, I'm afraid he will be able to see it in my expression.

My cheeks are burning as he lets go of my hand. He clears his throat.

"I was going to make a cup of tea, would you like one?"

"Yes please."

"A sandwich?"

I nod.

When I hear him filling the kettle in the kitchen I pull up the sleeve of my sweater and examine my wrist. I can't see anything, but it seems to me that I can still feel his grip and I flop backwards onto the bed, lie there on my back, close my eyes.

I dream of Stella that night. I am in a park full of green plants, no flowers, just dense, dark greenery: huge chestnut trees, cypresses, poplars, and silver fir, box clipped into tall walls and ivy creeping across the gravel on which I am standing, it is growing before my eyes, trying to reach my feet. It is twilight and the shadows are long, the air is raw and damp, it smells of fall, of decay.

Suddenly I see Stella's coffin on a bench a little way off, I hurry toward it, quickly, before the ivy has the chance to catch up with my feet, winding its way up my ankles and around my thighs. In my dream I know exactly how it feels, how tough the stems of the ivy are: long, strong fibers like ropes around my body, as if I have experienced it before. I can hear Stella's voice in my head, "That's poisonous, every part of it is poisonous," but ivy isn't poisonous, is it? Not in Sweden. I think I must ask her, and when I lift the lid of her coffin she is smiling at me and for a second it seems as if everything is a mistake, I have only dreamed that she is dead, but when I ask her she doesn't answer me. "Is it poisonous?" I say several times as I watch the ivy getting closer, she lifts one of her hands and her nails are long now, longer than mine. It isn't only hair that continues to grow after death, nails do too. I see Stella and Gabriel in my mind's eye, she drags her long nails down his back and he groans, takes hold of her wrists and presses his body hard against hers. Her hair is long too now, he could wind it around his hand, pull her head back, and the curls find their way over the sides of the coffin, crawling like the ivy, like the black roots of the alders in the lake, like shoots longing to find a foothold.

⎯⎯⎯

I have kicked off the covers in my sleep and I am so cold I am shivering when I wake up. Gabriel is sitting at the kitchen table drinking coffee and reading the newspaper, he nods to me when I walk in.

"Okay?" he mumbles.

"I didn't sleep too well."

I look out of the window as I pour coffee into one of the blue-and-white patterned cups that belonged to Gabriel's grandmother. It is beautiful old china, Swedish, from the beginning of the twentieth century. Gabriel has a complete service, he could serve eighteen people with several courses and still have enough. He uses the plates and cups every day, the rest is in a large display cabinet upstairs, pile upon pile of different-sized plates and serving dishes and a big soup tureen.

Outside the window the garden is gray and looks damp. Gabriel has hung some fat balls in a lilac bush that has lost all its leaves, and there are lots of little birds all around them. This is the same weather as we had for Stella's funeral, the weather has been the same all through the fall. Gabriel seemed distant then too, he hardly spoke to anyone, not even to me, nor I to him, I felt ashamed of myself afterward but I was afraid of his voice, it was so terrible to hear it: small and thick with tears, just as he sounded on the telephone that evening when he rang and told me she was dead, I was the first person he called.

"I think I'll go for a walk," I say.

"Mm."

He looks tired too, there are dark circles beneath his eyes and he is staring down at the paper without reading it.

Wet leaves stick to Stella's boots as I walk across the lawn. The great tits in the lilac bush take off in a flock as I approach, the air is full of the sound of their beating wings. I carry on out onto the gravel road, across the fields. One field has not been plowed like the rest, it is full of long grass that has turned yellow, it is wet and slimy. Perhaps it has been left to lie fallow. I clamber over the ditch and walk out onto it; after only a short distance it feels as if the landscape is endless, nothing but fields in front of me as far as the eye can see, a patchwork quilt, softly embedded in misty air. I close my eyes and turn my face up to the sky, it is quickly covered with a film of moisture.

As I am about to step back onto the gravel I see that there are rosehips growing in the ditch. They are beautiful, their red berries glowing against the black branches, and I think I might pick some, but there are too many thorns. I prick my forefinger as I try to snap off a twig and a bright-red drop of blood oozes out, I stick my finger in my mouth, the faint, clean, metallic taste of blood, of iron, rust. I should have brought a pair of pruning shears, there are some hanging in the hallway. Stella never left home without them.

I spin around as I hear footsteps on the road behind me. It's Anders with a dog on a lead, it is slender and dark gray, it might be a whippet. It slinks around his legs, looks at me attentively, sniffs the air. For a moment I imagine that it is picking up the scent of my blood, but my finger has stopped bleeding now.

"Hi," I say.

Anders nods to me. I clamber out of the ditch, almost slipping, I can't get any purchase on the long, wet grass with my boots.

"So you're out for a walk," he says.

"Yes."

I bend down to say hello to the dog, its breath is warm against my hand, but it doesn't want to be petted.

"I was sorry to hear about your sister."

He sounds kind, and he looks kind. I don't know what to say. He almost seems to regret having said anything, he is looking at me anxiously as if he's afraid I might start crying.

I straighten up.

"I'm here to sort out some of her things," I say.

"Not an easy job."

"No, it's very hard."

"You're very welcome to come over one day," says Anders. "You and Gabriel. Perhaps you could come over for coffee?"

I nod.

"Thank you . . . that would be nice."

"Give him my best."

"I will. Your tree is lovely, by the way."

He looks inquiringly at me.

"The apple tree . . . the one with the Christmas lights. We can see it from the upstairs window."

"Oh, that. Thanks."

He gives me a brief nod before setting off along the road. The dog dances and skips around his legs, gives a little yap at a bird in the wild rose bushes, it seems to be in a good mood.

I have trouble getting to sleep that night. It's windy again, it's always windy in the fall according to Gabriel, there's nothing to stop the wind whistling across the fields. It comes all the way from the sea, the sea I haven't yet seen except from far away when I was at the palace with Stella, glittering blue between the trees and bushes, the smell of salt and seaweed. I would like to go to the sea, I like being there in the fall, standing on a shore and gazing out across the endless expanse of gray, standing exactly on the waterline with Wellington boots on and letting the waves break over my feet if it's a calm day and the waves are small. It's a familiar scene, and yet I'm not sure it's a memory. When was I by the sea in the fall? On a sandy shore? I suddenly remember a visit to some friends of my parents when I was younger, perhaps only nine or ten years old. Stella was there too, it was a Saturday and she was furious because she had to come with us, she wanted to go into town with her girlfriends. I always imagined them trying on clothes, all three in the same cubicle, great piles of tops and jeans and skirts, giggling away and staying in there for ages, they were probably unbearable, but unbearable in a way I would have wanted to be too, along with them. It was fall, perhaps November like now, and our parents' friends lived by the sea, not right by the sea, but close enough to be able to see it from the upstairs windows of the old wooden house. We were having lunch, elk steaks, and Stella saw an opportunity to make a fuss about that too, she had no intention of eating elk, no way. The husband in the family used to hunt and I can remember the furrow on my mother's brow as she stared at Stella, that look clearly telling her not to start.

We went down to the sea after we'd eaten, Stella and I. She went on and on about the business of the elk, a poor innocent animal, she wanted me to agree with her, which I probably did even though I thought the elk steak was delicious. We had blackcurrant jelly with it, we never got that at home. There were rocks, low gray rocks sloping gently into the water and Stella went right down to the waterline, where the rocks were slippery and black with algae, as if she wanted to tease me, make me tell her to come away, not to go so near the edge, so that she could get cross with me too and snap at me, telling me I wasn't her mother. It had happened before and I didn't want it to happen again, not that afternoon, I wanted to be on Stella's side, so I said nothing even though I was so terrified that she would slip and fall into the water that I didn't dare take my eyes off her, not for a second.

⁓⊱✲⊰⁓

I wake up shivering, just as I do every morning, even though I have started sleeping with an extra blanket on top of the duvet. I wrap myself in the blanket as I pad across the hall floor and into the downstairs bathroom, take a long shower, the bathroom mirror is misted over and I draw a line with my forefinger. I think about when I was little, when it was winter and Stella and I were waiting in the backseat of the car for Mom and Dad, who had gone off to do some shopping or something, and the windows got all misted up on the inside and we drew flowers and animals and hearts, and Stella wrote the names of the boys she was in love with. Dad used to tell us to try not to breathe until he had closed the car door and we would laugh and try, timing each other to see how long we could hold our breath, Stella always won.

It was an accident, the police said, she was probably just testing out the temperature of the water. Maybe she slipped, banged her head. She was wearing her dress but was barefoot, perhaps she was just going to paddle in the shallow water where the rocks began, in the same spot where we went swimming in the summer, they sloped gently for quite a long way out into the water, you could walk on the smooth stone surface until the water came up to your thighs. Then it suddenly fell away steeply, and you had to start swimming. Was she surprised when the rock suddenly disappeared beneath her feet? Did she hit her head on the big rock just below the surface of the water? Not hard enough to cause a wound, but enough to make her dizzy, perhaps lose consciousness for a little while? Long enough to sink beneath the surface, it is deep where the rock falls away, the water is instantly colder. It doesn't matter how good you are at holding your breath if you're unconscious. The thought keeps on coming back, over and over again, was she conscious when she died? Did the colder water farther down make her come around, it must have been dark down there, perhaps it was difficult to work out which direction the light was coming from, which direction she ought to swim in? Did she try to swim? Even though she was running out of air? Did she have time to think anything?

I place the palm of my hand against the bathroom mirror, a blurred image of my face appears through the mist. I think about what Gabriel said on one of those first evenings back in the summer, that we weren't really alike, Stella and I. Not in appearance perhaps, I think. But we were both equally bad at swimming.

Gabriel is in town, he's gone to speak to his accountant and then he's going to do some shopping. He sounded surprised yesterday when I said I didn't want to go with him, but it's nice to have the house to myself. I have my breakfast in the living room while watching TV, drink my coffee in front of some stupid talk show, Gabriel hardly ever watches TV. Then I take two satsumas and another cup of coffee upstairs, walking carefully so that I won't spill any. It's warm at the desk on the balcony, even though it's so late in the fall. Presumably the balcony is better insulated than my bedroom, it's completely draft proof with chubby little radiators under some of the windows. Gabriel has made sure it's possible to work there all year round, although he has said he moves the computer into the bedroom if it gets too cold outside, it's so expensive to keep the balcony heated when that happens. But this is a long, mild fall, almost fifty degrees outside during the day and no frost at night, just gray air full of dampness.

I open my assignment on Gabriel's computer, it's only a few pages long. I scroll distractedly through the text thinking that it's bad, it's a bad choice of subject, it seems confused and slapdash and I've taken out books at random, I don't really know anything about existing research. I should have gone and looked up a few old newspaper articles—that always looks conscientious, or maybe just searched for books a little more carefully, this is never going to get me a pass. My tutor is nice but absentminded, there's no point in asking her for advice, she just keeps saying it all sounds very exciting. Perhaps I ought to ask Gabriel, but I don't like to bother him, and I'm afraid he'll be disappointed because I haven't worked harder. He got a book in the mail that he has to review and he's busy trying to find somewhere to live, an apartment he can borrow or rent. He's spent a lot of time on the phone, calling old friends, I hope he'll end up moving to Stockholm, that we'll be living in the same city.

I yawn, take a gulp of coffee out of the blue-and-white cup I have brought upstairs with me, type a sentence and immediately delete it. Outside the window everything is gray, I watch Nils moving slowly across the lawn, keeping his eye on the birds in the bushes. Leaves are whirling around him, wet and dark, the wind is much stronger now, the balcony windows are rattling. It always blows in the same direction here, off the sea and in across the fields, you can tell by the trees; they all bend slightly in toward the land, pointing east, like broken compass needles.

⸻

It is drizzling as I walk along the road across the field, I am wearing Stella's Wellington boots again. I would feel silly carrying an umbrella out here in the country, and my umbrella probably wouldn't have been much use anyway, it's cheap and flimsy, it turns inside out at the least gust of wind. Instead I have pulled Stella's dark-blue raincoat over my jacket and drawn the hood tight around my face. Inside it I feel cut off from the world, I can hardly see anything at the sides, and every sound is muted, as if I were underwater.

There is a tree in the graveled area in front of Anders and Karin's house, a chestnut, and I have to crouch down beneath it, breathing in the sweet scent and searching among the yellowish-brown fallen leaves, wet and slimy from the rain. Most of the chestnuts are losing their sheen and are damaged, chipped or cracked, but I find a spiky sphere that is still intact, covered in brown marks but undamaged, and I break open the tough shell until it gives way, peeling apart with perfect resistance, exposing a dark, shiny chestnut nestling in the soft white padding. I pick it out and slip it into my pocket, closing my hand around it; silky and cold and almost greasy against my palm, it feels good.

Anders opens the door almost immediately when I ring the bell. He's wearing a pair of scruffy jeans, spattered with both oil and paint, and a checked shirt. He looks pleased but surprised.

"Hey, look who's here!" he says.

"I just thought I'd . . ." I begin, but he interrupts me, shouts "Karin!," looks at me and nods.

"Good to see you," he says. "Come on in."

A woman appears in the hallway, she looks as if she's just over sixty, she's also wearing jeans, she looks youthful, well-cut shoulder-length hair without even a hint of gray. Perhaps she colors it, but she doesn't look the vain type. Maybe she's one of those naturally beautiful women I always envy; my hair is nondescript and mousy, so I color it a darker shade, I have to use an eyebrow pencil and mascara every day to stop me from feeling as if I'm disappearing. Maybe she doesn't even think about her hair, that's usually the case.

"'Look at the state of you," she says to Anders, nodding at his jeans, he gives an embarrassed smile.

"I wasn't expecting a visitor."

"I guess this is our neighbor," she says with a smile, shaking my outstretched hand energetically, and I start to explain again that I'm here because Anders invited me when I met him on the road, that's why I'm ringing their doorbell, but she doesn't seem to be listening, nor does she seem to think there's anything odd about the fact that I'm here. She takes my raincoat and puts it on a hanger over the bath, says that this is an unusual fall, so much rain and so mild.

"So where's the poet today?" says Anders.

I smile.

"He's at home working, he's got quite a bit on at the moment."

"Is it his new book?"

"No, that's finished. This is a review."

"Oh, so he does that kind of thing as well?"

"I'll make some coffee," says Karin.

We are sitting in a living room on the ground floor having our coffee, it's a small, cluttered room full of stuff: little tables with lamps and ornaments, big vases of dried flowers on the floor, plates and paintings and photographs on every wall and small crocheted mats all over the place, it looks older than Anders and Karin and I think maybe they inherited this house, along with the crocheted mats and everything else.

They talk mostly about the weather, about the area and about their dog, his name is Sture, apparently, after a dog in a children's book. He is lying at one end of the sofa on some cushions, he seems listless, barely reacting when I pat his head to say hello, I've never really known how to behave with dogs.

Anders and Karin have two children, a son and a daughter, their pictures are on the walls, from when they were christened and confirmed and when they graduated and got married. They've both moved to Stockholm, Karin tells me, but they come to visit at Christmas and Easter and sometimes for a few weeks in the summer, with their partners and children and dogs.

"Things get pretty lively around here then," says Anders, looking happy, I smile, thinking that I ought to visit my parents more often.

"They were here this summer," says Karin. "Although I don't think you were here then. They usually come at the beginning of July."

"No, I was here later," I murmur.

"Of course, that was before . . ." Karin says without finishing the sentence, but I can still hear the end in my head, "before Stella died," "before your sister drowned," "before it happened," it has become a fixed point in their frame of reference when it comes to time. Not much happens here, it's obvious that something like that will become significant, something everyone knows about and talks about, it was in the paper, it was front-page news.

"So how's he doing?" Anders says.

"Gabriel? Okay, I think."

Both Anders and Karin look concerned.

"So you're quite happy living there?" says Karin.

I don't understand what she means, but I mumble a yes and both she and Anders nod, relieved, and I suddenly realize it's not Gabriel they're worried about, it's me, and the fact that I'm living there with him. What do they really think of him? I wonder, then it occurs to me that perhaps they don't just think something, they know something, I suddenly feel sick, the coffee tastes sour. I want to ask a question but I don't know how to put it, Karin nods at me, encouraging me to take another cookie, there are several different kinds on the plate, all homemade: raspberry jelly, pearl sugar, chopped almonds, and I take one, chewing mechanically as Anders begins to talk about someone in the neighborhood whose cellar has been damaged by the rain, I look out of the window, twilight is already falling.

"It looks as if it's going to be Stockholm," Gabriel says that evening as we are sitting in the living room. This has become a habit now, like those evenings on the patio in the summer. Gabriel has made mulled wine, the first of the year. He seems delighted, he has even put out little bowls of raisins and almonds. The cat is fast asleep on the old wing chair, Gabriel has lit a fire in the tiled stove and we are sitting side by side on the sofa, close together.

"There's an apartment in the Söder area, it looks as if I'll be able to rent it for a year anyway."

He looks at me, smiling when he sees how pleased I am.

"For real?" I say, he laughs.

"For real. From the middle of December, so I'd better make a start on packing and sorting stuff out pretty soon."

I lean my head against his shoulder, feeling a great sense of relief spreading through my entire body, I close my eyes, I see myself visiting him, in an apartment in Stockholm. I wonder what he will take with him, whether he will take any books and if so which ones, whether the place is furnished or he will need his own furniture. In that case he would probably take the big old armchair in the living room, he sits in it when he's reading. And the floor lamp that stands beside it, it's from the thirties and has three shades made of pale-pink silk, like flowers, linnaea perhaps.

"I called in to see Anders and Karin," I say to Gabriel.

He nods. "They're nice people. Although we don't really hang out with them."

He stops himself.

"Didn't . . . we didn't hang out with them."

He rests his forehead on his hand, he looks exhausted.

"Would you have wanted to come with me?"

"No, I've got so much to do here."

He nods toward the book lying open on the table, a new edition of Rimbaud's poems in translation, he seems to be utterly absorbed by it, he talked about it over dinner too. It's been a long time since he wrote anything for the newspaper, although fall is high season for new publications. Stella used to nag him about making an effort to get more work, probably with some justification.

He reaches for the book.

"This really is incredibly good. Have you read Rimbaud?"

"No, I don't think so."

"You should."

He clears his throat, begins to read, his voice low but steady.

"On the calm black water where the stars are sleeping / White Ophelia floats like a great lily; / Floats very slowly, lying in her long veils. / In the far-off woods you can hear the call of the hunters."

He carries on reading, he seems almost hypnotized. I put my mulled wine down on the table, feeling uncomfortable. Gabriel looks at me.

"Isn't that beautiful?"

"No."

"It's such a lovely theme: beauty in death," he says quietly. "And the madness, the fact that she wants more than there is in this world, that life is not enough for her . . . and therefore she has to go under."

"There is nothing beautiful about death."

He's not listening.

"And the image of her when she's drowned, like a lily floating on the water in her pale dress, like a water lily."

I get up from the sofa.

"Where are you going?" he says.

"You're crazy," I mumble.

He looks surprised.

"Are we never going to talk about it?" I say. "Are we never going to talk about what we did to her and the fact that she's dead now, are we going to pretend it never happened?"

"But . . ." he begins.

"I don't understand how you can read that and just pretend nothing has happened."

"I'm not pretending nothing has happened," Gabriel says quietly.

"So how can you sit there and say it's beautiful? Because you actually think it's nice? The fact that she's not here to nag you anymore, so you can avoid taking responsibility for anything and just sit around reading poetry and being an artist?"

"Calm down, Marina."

His tone is sharper now.

"Was it you who forced her to make that mark on her leg?"

The question pops into my head from nowhere, but as soon as I've spoken I know it was the right thing to ask. I can see it in his eyes, a fleeting expression of surprise, I realize it's something he never thought I would ask.

"What do you mean?"

"I mean exactly what I said. She had a mark on her inner thigh, she said she'd burned herself with a cigarette. Was it you who made her do it?"

I have been feeling guilty about the mark on Stella's leg all through the fall, I didn't say anything about it during the police investigation. I hardly said anything at all, they didn't ask me many questions, I wasn't even there when it happened. In any case they should have noticed it themselves if they did an autopsy, they should have noticed it just from looking at her—and maybe they did, but they didn't mention it to Mom and Dad because they were being discreet, or maybe they did mention it but Mom and Dad didn't want to worry me. I can hear Mom's anxious voice in my head when the police call and someone asks her formally if Stella ever displayed any kind of self-harming behavior. Perhaps it was an experiment that went just a little too far—I picture her holding a glowing cigarette against the inside of her thigh, keeping it there as long as she can, she has decided on a fixed number of seconds, maybe in the same way as when she went down to the lake, maybe she'd decided to see how long she could hold her breath, just like when we were little, in the backseat of the car on those winter days, she tried to hold her breath for the same amount of time now, for as long as she could beneath the surface of the water, and then a little bit longer, just another ten seconds, I can see her in my mind's eye, pale, her face almost blue, she's not getting any air and she's enjoying it, just a little bit longer she thinks, her head is spinning, just a little bit longer and then everything goes black.

"Did she do it herself?" I say, since Gabriel doesn't speak.

"I don't know."

"Didn't you ask?"

"No. I don't actually know what you're talking about. You seem a bit confused, maybe you ought to go to bed."

I look him straight in the eye, and he holds my gaze. I don't recognize him at all, I don't want to be in the same room as him, he's lying, I think, for some reason he's lying. I leave him with the mulled wine in the living room, closing the door of my bedroom quickly behind me once I am inside.

Gabriel gets up early in the mornings now, he makes a big pot of coffee and pours it into a Thermos on the draining board. It's still piping hot when I get up around nine and stand at the kitchen window looking out over the wet gray late-fall garden, at a magpie on the black, tangled branches of the birch tree, the smaller birds on the fat balls in the lilac bushes. We have had the same weather every day since I got here, every day equally slow and gray, they flow somnolently into one another, all exactly the same, misty, mild, as if they were padded. Gabriel is writing, the house is silent. I sit at the kitchen table for a long time, I read the morning paper, a few lines in a book for my assignment, the same few lines over and over again. Gabriel appears in the kitchen at regular intervals to top up his coffee cup, nods good morning to me, asks me to let Nils in.

"How's it going?" I ask.

"Fine," he says absentmindedly, he's said the same thing every time I've asked. He's started writing something new, it might become a collection of short stories, he seems to be completely absorbed by it. He rummages around in the larder and finds a box of ginger cookies, grabs a handful and disappears up the stairs.

I take a walk around downstairs, I feel restless. There are still some of Stella's things to go through, boxes of papers from when she was at college, old assignments and notes, boxes of crockery and household bits and pieces she brought to the house with her but never even unpacked. I don't know what to do with all her stuff, I put it off, I can't bring myself to get rid of anything else right now, it feels wrong, as if I'm clearing her away, removing every trace of her.

It is dark in the living room. I switch on the big chandelier, it's too large for the room really, the ceiling isn't all that high. The light it gives is soft and warm, flattering. In a corner next to one of the bookcases is a bundle of old school posters with botanical motifs that Stella bought at an auction last summer, the dust swirls in the air as I leaf through them: potato, lingonberry, creeping thistle, a slender star-of-Bethlehem with elegant leaves, Stella loved alliums. Right at the back there is a poster of the spotted orchid, it is a pink flower. Suddenly I remember Stella's orchids in the greenhouse where she worked. Gabriel hasn't mentioned them, he hasn't said whether anyone is looking after them now, and when I think about it I realize Stella never said anything about them while he was around during the summer, even though she liked to talk about them. Does he even know they exist? He usually seemed to be listening with only half an ear when she talked about her plants, he seemed to like the fact that she was interested in them, even though he wasn't the least bit interested himself, particularly when she went into all the practical details about nutrition and fertilizer and pruning and different types of soil. Perhaps she told him about the orchids and he nodded, thinking about something else: his novel, himself.

There is a bus into town just after lunch, it's the same bus I caught in the summer when I was going to meet Stella. If I hurry I can catch it. I quickly put on some makeup and for the first time in ages pull on my own boots, it feels strange walking in heels after wearing Stella's flat Wellingtons for such a long time, I glance at my legs in the mirror, they look good.

"I'm going out for a while," I shout up the stairs to Gabriel, he responds with a preoccupied "Okay." I think that he probably wasn't even listening to what I said, and he'll wonder where I am the next time he comes down to fill up his coffee cup, but I haven't got time to write him a note, I'll miss the bus. I cut across the garden and run down the road, it's not so windy today and my umbrella is actually quite effective at keeping off the fine drizzle suspended in the air, it's almost motionless, like unusually wet mist.

When I switch on my CD player it skips at the beginning of the track I want to listen to, skips back to the start when it's played a few seconds, or jumps to a completely different track. I switch it off and on again several times, but it makes no difference. Maybe it's the dampness, the air is so wet all the time. I imagine everything inside it turning green, small copper wires and pins, all covered in a coarse green patina, I see it growing like salt crystals, making all the wires look furry, as soon as I get out into the damp air it's off, growing, multiplying, cutting out.

I reach the bus stop in plenty of time, the bus is almost empty, just like in the summer. It takes the same meandering, circuitous route as before, past farms where no one gets on and no one gets off and there is not a soul in sight, except for a cat sitting by a mailbox, black against the wet grass, and a big flock of jackdaws, silhouetted against the unchanging pale-gray sky.

When I get into town I can't find my way at first. Although the center is small I go wrong twice, in the end I have to ask a man who is cutting across the town hall square where the greenhouses actually are, he knows exactly, he points and explains. There are very few people about, the town almost feels deserted, and when I get to the greenhouses and press down the handle of the gate in the iron railings surrounding them, I discover it's locked. The cypresses beside the gateposts are dark with moisture, they look silent, serious.

I have been standing there for only a few minutes when a man riding a small moped pulls up behind me. The platform behind the moped is full of leaves and branches, the man is wearing bright-orange overalls.

"Are you waiting for someone?" he wonders.

"Yes, someone who can open the gate," I say, and he raises his eyebrows, no doubt wondering who I am. I realize I probably sounded rude.

"My sister used to work here," I say. "Stella."

His face softens immediately.

"We all miss her," he says as he fishes out a bunch of keys from one of his pockets.

"Mm."

"Not like you, of course," he adds hastily.

I follow him along the gravel path and into the greenhouse. It is warm inside, the heat is even more noticeable than it was in the summer, but now the humidity is almost as high outside as inside the greenhouse. The man in the orange overalls waves to a woman in an oversized men's shirt, the same kind of clothes Stella used to wear when she was working in the greenhouses. Her blonde hair is caught up in a knot at the back of her neck.

"This is Stella's sister," says the man in the overalls, and the blonde woman introduces herself as Linda, she also tells me they miss Stella and offers her condolences and says how tragic it all was, I swallow and nod.

"Have you come to pick up her things?"

I shake my head.

"No . . . no, not now. I just wondered how the orchids were getting on."

I realize this sounds odd, confused probably, but Linda smiles kindly at me and invites me to accompany her to the corner where the orchids are growing.

Some of them are still flowering, they look exactly the same as they did in the summer, that same unreal, almost waxy perfection. I place the palm of my hand on the damp moss, it feels good. The air is sweet, with a powdery scent, it immediately makes me think of that summer afternoon and how annoyed I got with Stella when she insisted I was late meeting her from work, what did it matter, I feel stupid when I think about it now.

"We've looked after them," says Linda. "You don't need to worry."

I nod.

"She was so proud of them," I say, and then my voice breaks and I am on the verge of tears.

Linda places her hand on my arm, tells me to sit down on a little bench over by the wall and I do as

I am told, I sit there watching Linda as she fetches a small trowel and a plant pot, lifts a small piece of the moss surrounding one of the flowering orchids and pushes the trowel into the soil underneath. She takes her time, gently loosening the roots, teasing and poking until the pink flower and all its tangled roots are free. Then she piles soil into the pot, carefully inserts the orchid, makes sure it's standing firm. When she has moistened the soil and smoothed a piece of shiny, velvety moss over it, she hands the pot to me.

"Here."

"Thank you," I say quietly, my voice holds now.

The orchid in the pot looks as if it's gaping at me openmouthed, the flower head looks too heavy for the thin stem. I have never really liked orchids, I think there's something faintly revolting about them, they are so palpably organic.

"Are they parasites?" I ask.

Linda smiles.

"No. They're epiphytes, it's not the same thing. They grow in trees, but they don't suck nutrition from them. They just use the trees to climb higher up, to get at the light."

I nod.

"It can be very dark down on the floor of the rain forest," she adds. "There are so many trees and leaves that it's not so easy for the flowers. Would you like a drink?"

"Yes please."

I follow her through the greenhouse, past rows of hyacinths and amaryllis to the far end, past the little pond with the babbling water where the two carp slowly glide around like black shadows, then through a door leading to an untidy office. There is a table and some chairs in one corner and she nods, inviting me to sit down. I am still holding the plant pot in my hand, it is cool, silky smooth. Linda clatters around in a small kitchen area, I can see her through a swaying curtain made of brightly colored plastic beads, her movements make the beads rattle. I put down the pot containing the orchid on the table. I can smell coffee. Linda places a yellow mug in front of me.

"Milk, sugar?"

"No, it's fine . . . thanks."

She sits down opposite me, takes a sip of coffee from an identical mug.

"How are things?" she says.

She seems as if she really wants to know, unlike Gabriel, who asks me all the time without showing any interest in my answer. Although I do exactly the same, I think, I let him get away with "fine" every time I ask how things are going.

"I was thinking about the old containers," I say. "Stella told me about them in the summer, she'd found them in a storeroom somewhere. Old containers for plants, they looked like leaves, kind of . . . instead of those white plastic ones."

Linda nods.

"I've already sorted it," she says. "They're going to be on the bridge and in the pedestrian area, we'll be putting them out at Easter, they're going to look fantastic. Have you seen them?"

I shake my head.

"Come with me and I'll show you."

Gabriel appears in the hallway as soon as I walk through the door.

"Where have you been?"

"In town."

I put down the orchid on the bureau in the hall, sit down on the wooden chair next to it, and pull off my boots.

"You've been gone for such a long time."

He both looks and sounds agitated.

"But I told you I was going out."

"I had no idea when you'd be home. I'm making dinner, it's Friday, remember."

His words sound so practiced that I think that's how he must have sounded when he was talking to Stella, maybe this is a discussion he's had before, but with her. As if all I have to do is slip into the role. She told me they usually had a special dinner on Friday night, and that he always did the cooking, she used to say she was lucky to have found a man who could cook.

"Sorry," I say. "Do you want some help?"

His expression immediately grows softer, almost tender.

"Just some company."

I follow him into the kitchen, it smells good, I realize I'm hungry. He has lit candles on the table and in the window, and I can hear the crackling of the wood in the tiled stove from the living room. He pours me a glass of wine.

"A toast," he says, handing me the glass.

"To what?"

He smiles.

"I don't know. To you?"

"Me?"

He shrugs his shoulders.

"Well, me then?"

"Your book?"

"No, that's too boring. Taste the wine."

I laugh and obey him. It's a delicious wine, silky and served at the perfect temperature, the bottle is standing next to the cooker, where it's warm from the oven. I sit down at the kitchen table and watch him as he puts the finishing touches on dinner. He looks self-assured in everything he does, every little movement.

As a starter he has made mushroom soup from yellow foot chanterelles. He tells me that he and Stella picked them last autumn, they found this fantastic place and picked several bagfuls. I picture them sitting on the patio cleaning the mushrooms when they got home, spreading newspaper over the table and tipping them all out, a little yellow-and-brown mountain, then starting to clean them, picking out all the needles and lingonberries and leaves, brushing and wiping as confused little insects and spiders tumbled down onto the newspaper and crawled away across the table. It was probably one of those clear, sunny days, one of those perfect October afternoons with sunshine and crisp air and beautiful colors on the trees.

The main course is a casserole of elk meat and bacon, the sauce is dark, Gabriel serves it with a potato gratin cut into squares and a salad of small, pretty leaves with red veins, some kind of dressing drizzled over them, the dressing is dark too, it's like something you would get in a restaurant.

"That looks wonderful."

Gabriel smiles, pours more wine into my glass.

"You must taste the meat . . . I bought it from Anders, he hunts. It's usually fantastic."

The meat is tender and must have been stewing for a long time, absorbing the dark sauce, which is full of flavor, the wine complements it perfectly.

"It's awesome."

Gabriel laughs and mimics me, he likes to tease me, he thinks it's funny that I say "awesome," he tells me I sound as if I'm about fourteen. He tops up my glass again, he has opened another bottle. I feel calm now, pleasantly relaxed and slightly drowsy from the wine, it's raining outside, hammering on the window ledges. It's warm in the kitchen, and in the living room when we eventually move, sitting on the sofa and drinking more wine. Gabriel has opened the outer brass doors of the tiled stove, and the thin black doors inside, until only the innermost doors remain closed, sooty and dark with a pattern of holes allowing the glow to shine through in a patchwork of warm orange dots, crackling softly.

We are sitting close together, so close that I can rest my head on his shoulder, he is wearing a shirt and a lamb's wool sweater, he knows I like him in it. I am faintly aware of his smell, I think vanilla is the most reassuring smell. Like something from when I was a child.

He strokes my hair, a little absentmindedly at first, then he asks me to undo the loose knot I have gathered up at the back of my neck.

"Why?"

"You look so lovely with your hair down."

I loosen the band holding the knot together and my hair falls down around my shoulders, he reaches out and adjusts it, arranges it on either side of my face, gazing at me with a serious expression.

"You really are beautiful," he says quietly.

His eyes are dark now, he gets up from the sofa.

"Come with me," he says, and I follow him, through the living room and the kitchen and up the stairs, I have to hold on to the banister, I can tell I'm drunk now.

It is dark in the bedroom. He switches on the old lamp on the table at his side of the bed, it has a brass base with an ornate pattern, the shade is made of pale-green velvet with a gold fringe, the light is muted. Through the balcony window I can see Anders and Karin's apple tree, slightly blurred by the rain, it sparkles all night.

Gabriel opens the door of one of the closets and takes out a dress. It is black and embroidered with small beads, it has thin shoulder straps, it looks expensive. When I see the label on the back I realize it must have been, it says Prada. I look at him.

"What's that?"

"I bought it for Stella when we were in Italy."

"It's gorgeous."

"You should try it on."

"What?"

I feel as if my brain is working very slowly. Gabriel smiles at me, pulls down the zipper at the side of the dress.

"You'd look so lovely in it. With your hair exactly like that. It's such a pity to have it hanging there practically unworn."

He holds out the dress to me, smiles, nods toward the folding screen next to the closet. It's old, it wasn't Gabriel's grandparents who bought it but some relative long ago, it's made of wood, with a glossy black lacquer finish, patterns of Asiatic fish with fins like veils, billowing aquatic plants in gold and green. I look at the fish as I get changed, it almost seems as if they are moving, winking at me, I think of the carp in the pond in the greenhouse, their slow movements under the water, I carefully pull on the dress. It is lined with soft silk, it slips easily over my body, it feels cool. It's almost like diving, I think, like being enveloped by water. I can see myself in the mirror on the wall. It really is a beautiful dress, the most expensive thing I've ever had on, and it fits perfectly, I must have lost weight. Stella was always slightly slimmer than me, a little shorter and thinner, her clothes were always half a size too small when I wanted to borrow them, nothing ever fitted quite right. My lips are darker than usual, from the wine, I moisten them, smile tentatively at my reflection.

Gabriel is sitting on the bed, I hear him take a deep breath as I step out from behind the screen.

"Come here," he says quietly and I obey, crossing the bedroom floor until I am standing in front of him and he touches the fabric of the dress, gently runs his hand over my thigh, looks up at me.

"You are so beautiful," he murmurs.

His hand is on my thigh again, he draws me a little closer, parts his legs so that I am standing between them, he strokes the back of my thigh and slides his hand upward, I close my eyes, breathing more heavily. He is touching me with both hands now, outside the fabric, then suddenly inside, I gasp as I feel his hands on my skin, softly caressing my thighs, then all at once they are groping toward the back, up beneath the dress, more determined now.

He puts his hands around my waist, I bend down and he puts them around the back of my neck instead, pulling my head toward his, he kisses me and I part my lips, his mouth tastes of wine. I gently draw my nails down the nape of his neck, under the collar of his shirt and he groans, pulls me down onto the bed, on my back. He lies on top of me and carries on kissing me, he touches my hair, gathers it into a bunch, winds it around his hand, he grips my wrist with the other hand, the way he did in the greenhouse last summer, the way he did a few days ago when he was looking at my nail polish, his grip is just as firm now and he is still kissing me, pulling my head back and then letting go of my hair,

running his hand the length of my body instead,
over my breasts and my waist, over my thighs, then
under my skirt again. I groan, press myself against
him, his hands are inside my panties now, he moans
as he feels how wet I am.

"Oh my God," he murmurs, both surprised and
aroused, as if he doesn't believe it's true, he has to feel
again, feel more, I press myself against his hand and
he moves it back and forth, I whimper, cling to him,
my hands inside his shirt now, I drag my nails down
his back and he groans even more loudly, moves his
hand faster between my legs, I have stopped thinking,
I am conscious of nothing but his hand. I fumble for
the button of his jeans, I find it but can't get it un-
done, he lets go of my wrist to help.

"Get on all fours," he says quietly and when I don't
obey immediately he says it again, more sharply this
time, I do as he says and he is behind me, touching
me outside the dress at first and then inside, he pushes
it up, pulls my panties to one side.

Gabriel has started packing, he lets me use his computer during the day. He's out a lot, getting things
sorted, he's got a lot of stuff to get rid of. He takes
several carloads to the dump, and boxes and boxes to
a charity, they organize flea markets in the summer,
he takes all of Stella's things there, books and records

and magazines. He says he never really managed to sort out his grandparents' things when he moved into the house, he just pushed it all into boxes and stored it in the toolshed in the garden, which was already full of boxes they had put there. Now he unpacks them all and goes through the contents, sorting everything out, it keeps him busy for several days. He packs most of it to be given away, but finds a few things he wants to hold on to, he comes to show me when he finds something he likes, he looks happy, as if he has discovered a treasure: old china figurines, books, a box full of poetry by authors I've never heard of, Gabriel waves several of the collections at me triumphantly, tells me they are first editions, they are valuable. He's going to take them with him to Stockholm, he says, and packs them into a different box, he's going to take a lot of books even though he says he's taking only the most essential, there are huge gaps on the bookshelves in the living room now.

"How's it going?" he says, sneaking a look at the computer screen, I scroll down the page, I don't want him to read it.

"Oh, not too bad," I mumble. "I've written a few pages."

He stands behind me, gently stroking my hair, his expression preoccupied as he gazes out across the fields. Twilight is falling, the sun sets early and the wind has got up over the past few days, the clouds are torn to shreds, ragged pink-and-orange clouds glowing on the horizon against the background of the dark sky before the sun disappears completely. Gabriel has bought some hyacinths, two of them are on the balcony and are half out, one pink and one purple, there is already a faint scent in the air.

"It's cold in your room, isn't it?" he says.

I look up at him.

"Yes."

"There's more of a draft downstairs," he says. "The windows are older."

He looks at me, seems to be searching for the right words.

"I've been thinking . . . you can sleep up here with me if you want. I mean, it's so windy at the moment, it's stupid for you to lie there freezing at night."

I don't know what to say, I merely nod in response, but at bedtime I take my duvet and pillow upstairs, make up the bed with my sheets on Stella's side and crawl in, waiting for Gabriel to come to bed, beneath the shadows cast on the ceiling by the apple trees in the garden.

It is Gabriel's turn to choose a record as we sit in the living room the following evening. He has several crates of vinyl LPs, but he says he has sold at least as many, he regrets it now but he needed the money to pay his rent one summer, it was when he was a student and had just moved to Stockholm. He picks out an album and passes the sleeve to me, I look at it distractedly. The living room smells of hyacinths too now, there are hyacinths on virtually every windowsill, filling the entire house with their perfume. My head feels woolly, it's felt like that for several days now, I just push things out of my mind; this is the result of not finishing my assignment, of dropped points and the threat of my student loan being withdrawn, it's too hard, I just avoid thinking about it. This morning I looked up Rossetti's *The Annunciation* in one of the art books I have with me, his Mary doesn't look afraid at all, the way I remembered her. She looks as if her mind is somewhere else, she looks determined, as if she is convincing herself that what is taking place in front of her isn't really happening. I think we are very much alike, Mary and Marina.

We are drinking tea, Gabriel has laid out a proper little tea party: scones and small jars of jelly, he seems elated, he talks about how good he thinks it will be to get away from here for a while. He doesn't even know if he wants to come back for the summer anymore, he says, he's wondering about renting out the house, going abroad instead, staying somewhere for a long time and doing some writing.

"Sweden is too small for me," he says with a laugh.

I make an effort to smile in response.

"You can come and visit me, of course!" he says.

"Where will you go?" I say, I can hear how thin my voice sounds. He doesn't appear to notice.

"To France, probably. Or Italy, I've hardly spent any time in Italy . . . except when . . . well, except when I was there with Stella. Have you?"

I shake my head.

"I've hardly been anywhere."

I had gotten used to the idea that Gabriel would be living in Stockholm, I'd started to like it, to like the thought that he would be there when I needed someone who understood, without my having to explain and defend everything. I've even thought about sleeping with him in Stockholm too, but now that evening back in the summer feels much too close again, the evening after he had kissed me for the first time and it seemed to me that it was all a game to him. Perhaps it still is. And it still isn't a game to me, however much I might want it to be, I knew that the very first night I lay next to him in bed, when he had fallen asleep and I was lying there listening to his breathing and I felt safe, for the first time in an eternity. It has never been a game to me.

I have to blink away the tears, I can't keep crying all the time, over everything, crying is all I have done these past few months, I have cried until I was sick, or until I fell asleep through sheer exhaustion, my body weary and heavy, shaking, feverish. I have to stop crying at some point.

I pick at a tattered price ticket on the record sleeve, look at the photo of the band on the back. The lighting is dramatic, they all have spiky hair and jackets with huge shoulder pads, they look deadly serious, even now after twenty years, even though I should think most people who see this picture will be laughing at them now.

"What did you look like in the eighties?" I ask Gabriel, changing the subject.

He laughs, he doesn't seem to have noticed that his comments about moving abroad have upset me.

"Oh, I was young and handsome in the eighties. And I wore some terrific jackets."

"And did you have a terrific hairstyle?"

"There was nothing wrong with my hairstyle."

He smiles.

"I've got some photos somewhere . . . if I can find them. And if you're interested?"

"Sure."

He gets up and pulls out several drawers in the large bureau in the living room before he finds what he's looking for: a pile of large black photo albums. He flicks through them to sort out the chronology, then hands me the one he has decided is the earliest.

"That must be eighty-two, eighty-three, some-thing like that," he says, sitting down beside me on the sofa again, looking over my shoulder as I open the album and smile at a very young Gabriel in a striped jacket and narrow black trousers. There are pictures from a party at the beginning, Gabriel says it was when he first moved to Stockholm and started studying. In one of the pictures he has his arm around the shoulders of a blonde girl with a lot of black makeup around her eyes, in another he is kissing her. On the next page they are stand-ing in a square in what looks like southern Europe, the buildings in the background are beautiful but shabby, the facades flaking, the palm trees casting long shadows across the cobbles in the square, Ga-briel is screwing up his eyes at the camera and the blonde girl is wearing big, dark sunglasses.

"That was in Spain," says Gabriel. "Her name was Åsa."

In the next album Gabriel's hair is a little longer and he is dressed almost entirely in black, he sits smoking at café tables, some in Stockholm, some in Copenhagen, Paris, Rome, he did a lot of trav-eling at one time he tells me, sometimes with a friend but usually alone, one album later it's '88, '89, Gabriel has moved to Paris, he's wearing a white shirt and a black jacket, his hair is even lon-ger, he's usually unshaven and there is a beautiful young woman next to him in many of the pictures. She has long dark hair, straight and shiny, dark eyes, a coat that is tightly belted around her waist, it has a big fur collar, she is smiling at the camera in almost every picture.

"That's Adèle," says Gabriel, and I nod.

"She's very beautiful."

"Yes. She is."

He gets up again, goes over to one of the windows and seems to be looking out, even though it's too dark outside for him to be able to see anything but his own reflection. He places the palms of his hands on the windowsill and sighs.

"It must be ten years since I last looked at those pictures."

I turn the pages, they're having a picnic now, it's summer. Adèle is sitting on a blanket and smiling at the camera, she's wearing a striped vest top and a white skirt. Then there are several party pictures, Gabriel with a cardboard fez on his head and a glass in his hand, grinning, Adèle sitting cross-legged on an Oriental rug.

"Are you okay?" I say.

Gabriel shakes his head over by the window.

"I don't know. It just feels like such a long time ago. I feel . . . old, I guess."

He turns and gives me a wan smile.

"I think I'll have another cup of tea," he says. "Would you like one?"

"Yes please."

He disappears into the kitchen with our teacups as I carry on looking through the album: Adèle's birthday, she is laughing and blowing out the candles on a cake, I try to count them and I make it twenty-two, Gabriel and Adèle on a balcony, she's in a toweling robe and there is a plate of toast in front of her, Gabriel and Adèle on a jetty, it looks as if it's somewhere in the Swedish archipelago, birch trees in the background, Gabriel has rolled up his jeans and is unshaven, he looks tired in the bright light, suddenly significantly older than in the pictures in the early albums. Then Adèle getting ready to go out somewhere, trying on shoes in front of a full-length mirror, she is wearing thick eyeliner and a black dress, I peer at the picture. The dress has narrow shoulder straps, it ends just above the knee, it looks expensive. I know that it is lined with soft silk, that it is embroidered with tiny black beads even though you can't see them in the photograph, I know it feels cool against your body when you slip it on, I know that the fabric is thin but falls beautifully thanks to the weight of the beads.

I swallow. Gabriel places a steaming cup of tea on the table in front of me, I jump, quickly turn the page, but change my mind and turn back.

"This . . ." I say, I realize as soon as I begin to speak that I have no idea what to say. "This is the dress."

I point at the picture of Adèle, Gabriel frowns, looks at me inquiringly.

"The one you had in the closet? The one you said you'd bought for Stella?"

I look at him searchingly, his face is expressionless.

"The one you told me to put on . . . you remember?" I say faintly, but he shows no indication of understanding what I'm talking about. He puts his teacup down next to mine.

"It's not the same dress," he says.

I point to the photograph again.

"But it is, I can see that."

I'm convinced that I'm right now, my voice is stronger.

"Why did you say you'd bought it for Stella?"

"It's not the same dress," Gabriel says again, he looks a little annoyed now, but mostly tired, weary. "It's very similar, you're right there. But it's not the same."

I get up from the sofa.

"I'll go and get it, then we can compare."

He shakes his head.

"Sit down, Marina," he says. "I don't even have it anymore."

"What?"

"I took it to the charity place with the rest of Stella's things."

"But why?"

He shrugs his shoulders.

"Did you want it?"

"What are you up to?"

He looks at me, he really doesn't seem to understand what I'm talking about. He's a good liar, I think, maybe even better than me, but then he is a writer, that's his job.

Gabriel hums along to the music, looks at me.

"Don't you want your tea?"

I shake my head.

"And you don't want my company either?"

I feel revolted, almost nauseous.

"No," I mumble, I am already halfway to the kitchen, leaving him sitting by the table in the living room.

But when he comes upstairs later and gets into bed I have to cuddle up to him once more, I went to bed before him, I lay and read for a while, thinking that I would fall asleep before he came up, and if I hadn't fallen asleep I would pretend I had, I would sleep with my back to him. But then I smell him and my stomach contracts, the scent of vanilla, and I have to move closer, lay my cheek against his chest and feel the calmness spreading through my whole body as I listen to the beating of his heart. He tips my face back and kisses me gently and then I begin to cry, and he wipes away my tears and puts his arms around me and I want him to kiss me again, so he does, more hungrily this time, he kisses my cheeks too and his lips taste of salt and I cling to him.

"I don't want you to go and live in a different country," I whisper. "I want to be with you."

I am still crying, he strokes my hair, it feels like the evening I arrived, that very first evening on the sofa when he consoled me and I fell asleep with my head on his chest.

"Of course we'll be together," Gabriel murmurs. His hand has slid down over my hair and down my back, down to my thigh, he is stroking it in a way which is both soft and firm at the same time, up and down, slipping under my nightdress. I am aroused by his touch even though I am still crying, my head suddenly feels tender, feverish, I hold him tightly. Secrets bind people together, I think, perhaps he has also realized that now, that guilt is like a tie, that we are joined together now, his kisses taste more strongly of salt and suddenly I can barely remember why I am crying anymore, I am aware of nothing but his hand against my thigh, of course we'll be together, I think, who else would we be with.

Every day the same mist, the same rain. We go to visit the palace, it's Gabriel's idea. At first we were just going to go to the nearest little store to buy food, something we needed for dinner, tomatoes and basil and more satsumas for me, but then neither of us wanted to go back home.

From a distance it looks like a stage set, or a silhouette, the palace with its two wings highlighted against the flat pale-gray sky, the avenue of trees, the trees in the park, black and wet, the mist hanging like curtains in the air. Gabriel hasn't been there since that first fall with Stella, I think of what she said about coming back at the same time of year. It is a different season now, with rain that never stops, mist that never lifts. Gabriel holds my hand as we walk along the avenue, the stones on the ground crunching beneath our feet, the gravel is wet and dark, mixed with the remains of thousands of chestnuts and their outer shells. His hand is warm, it feels big in mine, I squeeze it hard, thinking it is like a promise, even if there is no one there to witness it.

The café is closed now, no one comes here on a weekday at this time of year. There is a notice advertising a Christmas market on the weekends, there is straw outside a little shed by the entrance, perhaps someone sits in there making traditional decorations like Christmas goats and sheaves of wheat for the birds and stars made of straw to hang on the tree, but the only sign of Christmas is the Advent candles in the window of the palace, they are lit when twilight begins to fall. We wander around the gardens for a while, a man who is putting up lights in a tree nods to us, it occurs to me that he thinks we're a couple, I wonder briefly if he recognizes Gabriel. Most people around here seem to recognize him, perhaps the man in the garden thinks I am Stella, I am wearing her raincoat. I squeeze Gabriel's hand harder, he squeezes back, looks at me and smiles.

⁓⋆⊰❁⊱⋆⁓

I ought to go out walking more often, I think as I pull the raincoat hood more tightly around my face, I would like to go somewhere else for once, but there is nowhere else to go: across the fields or along by the forest, but that only takes you down to the lake, and I don't want to go there. And yet I head in that direction, turning off to the left of the gravel road instead of the right, as you would do if you were going to the lake; I find myself surrounded by wet, dark pine trees, battered by year after year of wind, they have been unable to grow tall and straight but have been flattened down instead, grown short and strong, they look almost stylized, like something from a symbolist painting. They look out of place among the beech and oak, the needles crunch softly beneath my feet, sodden and shiny, the roots of the pine trees by the path are also shiny, slippery with the rain. There is a faint aroma of pine resin in the air, the last time I smelled it was in the summer, the scent of warm forest, summer forest, when I had been down to the lake, and when Stella and I had been there, on the path through the forest.

That was her last walk, along the path on the other side of the gravel road. She must also have been conscious of the smell of warm forest that afternoon, the weather stayed hot well into late summer, she was wearing a dress. She was wearing a dress when they pulled her out of the lake. She hadn't been there long, she didn't look as horrible as she does in my mind. Not like in films when they pull a body out of a lake. I've read about it, what happens to the body after death, I've read revolting details even though I don't really want to know, but nothing like that happened to her, there wasn't time, she just looked as if she'd been sitting in the bath for too long, as if she'd fallen asleep as the bathwater cooled, as if she'd gotten cold, her lips pale, the tips of her fingers wrinkled. I want to push the thought away, I don't want to think about it anymore, not again, I don't want to think about Stella, not like that.

I can see something bright red moving a short distance away in the forest, it takes a moment for me to realize it's a person: shapeless, shiny. It's Karin, in a big red raincoat that surrounds her like a tent. She's out for a walk with Sture, he slips beneath the ferns like a shadow, sniffs at a tree in passing, seems to be on his guard.

Karin smiles when she catches sight of me.

"Out for a walk?"

"Yes . . . I don't really know my way around the forest, but I just wanted to go somewhere different for once."

She nods.

"You can't get lost here. There are main roads in two directions and the sea in the third."

She waves her hand, presumably in the direction of the sea; I think it's over to the west.

"A cup of coffee would go down very nicely right now," she says.

I nod.

"Definitely."

"You will come back to the house with us?" she says, and I realize her comment about the coffee was an invitation.

"Oh . . . yes please, that would be great."

. . .

Karin tells me that Anders is in town doing some shopping, she chats away as she makes the coffee in the kitchen, asking if I would prefer cookies or a sandwich. She gives Sture some food in an old china dish, he gobbles it down and it occurs to me that this is the first time I've seen him show any enthusiasm about anything.

We sit in the living room again, Karin has to switch on the main light. She says it gets dark so early now, and then there's the constant rain, it never gets properly light, not even in the middle of the day. The room feels peaceful, there isn't a sound apart from the soporific drumming of the rain on the window ledges, all the ornaments and framed photographs so neatly arranged on their little crocheted mats, not a speck of dust. A small group of china dogs stands on the bureau, all the same breed as Sture. Karin notices me looking at them.

"I've been collecting them since I was young. Although I still haven't found all that many."

She smiles, changes the subject and starts talking about her sister who lives in Spain, in Alicante. She and Anders are going to visit her in January, as they usually do. Then it seems as if she feels she has said something inappropriate, and at first I don't understand what it is, but then I realize that she thinks the word "sister" might be too difficult for me, that she's afraid of upsetting me.

"It's okay," I say to her, she nods, takes a deep breath.

"Things can't have been too easy for her," she says.

"What do you mean?"

"For your sister. Living with him."

"Gabriel?"

She nods again.

"Didn't she say anything about it?" she asks.

"About what?"

"How they used to quarrel?"

"No?"

Karin shakes her head.

"I suppose she didn't want to worry you."

"I don't understand. Worry me about what?"

I have put down my coffee cup now.

"Well, we had our suspicions that things weren't quite right," she says. "And then she came over here once . . ."

"Who, Stella?"

". . . and she was absolutely beside herself, she was crying, and she said . . . well, she said he'd hit her."

"I don't believe you."

"They'd had such a terrible quarrel, she was virtually hysterical."

"No."

Karin looks at me in surprise.

"I thought she'd told you this."

I shake my head.

"It isn't true."

I feel sick, shaky, perhaps it's the coffee, or the cold, I want to close my eyes and put my hands over my ears and vanish from the sofa and the table and the plate of cookies, they are dry, crumbly cookies, my jaws crunch them mechanically, I take a swig of coffee to force them down.

"Oh yes it is," I hear Karin say, she sounds resigned but firm at the same time. "It's tragic, certainly, but it's definitely true."

"When . . . when was this?" I say, my voice sounds small and weak now.

"It must have been about a year ago. It was last fall."

I don't like coming home to a dark house, I get annoyed with Gabriel when he doesn't leave a couple of lamps lit in the windows, he never thinks about that kind of thing. He likes the dark, he thinks it's unnecessary when I go around turning on the lights, switching on the lamps upstairs even though no one is there, I have said I find it unpleasant walking up the stairs toward solid darkness, he just laughs, says I'm being silly, overdramatic.

I hurry home from Anders and Karin's, there are no lights along the gravel road either, but my night vision is good. I follow the edge of the road without any problem, pull the raincoat more tightly around me, it keeps out the wind but not the cold.

Nils is sitting on the steps waiting for me, he meows demandingly as I scrabble for the key in the deep pockets of the raincoat, slinks in quickly as soon as I open the door. Perhaps I ought to ask Gabriel about Advent candles, I think. Perhaps there is a box of Christmas decorations somewhere. There isn't really much point in putting anything up, since we will both be leaving soon, but perhaps a few candles in the windows, they could be left burning, glowing when we get home.

When I have switched on some lights down below I go upstairs, virtually every step creaks. It is dark up there. I quickly turn on the ceiling light on the little landing, the floor creaks there too. In the bedroom the apple trees are casting their shadows on the sloping ceiling as usual, I switch on the main light to chase them away, sit down on the bed, on Stella's side, which is mine now, open the drawer of the bedside table. Her diary is still there, the silk cover shining as I take it out. About a year ago, last fall. I flick back through the pages, past notes about my visit, midsummer celebrations with friends, the spring planting,

Christmas, I notice my initial again but I don't want to stop and read.

The descriptions of last fall are equally sparse. There are notes about meetings with Christmas groups and budgets, weekend outings, the trivia of everyday life, they buy a new coffee machine because Stella has broken the pot belonging to the old one, they see a film she thinks is excellent, Nils has been in a fight and doesn't seem very well, they take him to the vet, he quickly gets better, I glance through the pages until I reach August and summer without anything in particular having happened, apparently, and then I start again, thinking about what Karin said. I read more carefully this time, Thursday, October 18, *Sometimes I get annoyed when G doesn't seem to be working, even though he says he is—I ought to just leave it, mentioned it to L at work. She said as long as he has money, it doesn't really matter, does it? No doubt she's right,* Tuesday, October 23, *The sweep was supposed to come and check the chimney but G has been out twice when he turned up. I didn't want to light the fire tonight, I don't like it when it doesn't feel safe, but G insisted. Thought I could smell burning all evening.*

Is there an undertone of frustration in these brief notes, or am I imagining things? How would I have read them if I had been sure everything was fine between Stella and Gabriel? I imagine the scene with the chimney sweep, as Stella tells Gabriel he can surely take some responsibility given that he's home all day, he replies that he's working, that he went out for a walk, surely he's allowed to go out for a walk, he forgets things when he's in the middle of a novel, Stella snorts, mumbles something about the fact that he's been in the middle of this particular novel for a hell of a long time now. Then he lights a fire in the tiled stove, even though she asks him not to. Perhaps she says "What if the chimney catches fire!," he says it hasn't so far, you don't need to have the chimney swept as often as the sweeps say anyway, of course there's a margin, of course they say it needs to be done frequently, that's how they make their living after all. Perhaps she is having one of those days when she's easily provoked, easily hurt or annoyed, perhaps she says "Well I have no intention of being here if you're going to light the fire," he says "Suit yourself," she goes into the hallway, pulls on her boots and raincoat, goes out, where does she go?

Or maybe it wasn't like that at all. Maybe it was just like when I asked Gabriel to leave the lamps on, he said "That's not really necessary," I said I thought it was unpleasant, coming home to a dark house, he smiled, said "Silly girl" in a tone of voice that was kind, even loving, but at the same time made it clear that he had no intention of leaving any lamps on, and that I would just have to put up with it.

"Can't you smell burning?" I imagine her saying to him, he laughs, says "Silly girl" in that kindly tone of voice. Perhaps I should have stuck to my guns with the lamps, I think. Not let him end the discussion by calling me silly.

I pick up the diary again. Wednesday, November 11, *My hair has been a mess for such a long time now, I was going to have it cut tomorrow, I wanted quite a bit taken off. Gabriel wouldn't hear of it.* There is nothing the following day about how things turned out. I try to remember whether Stella had her hair cut or not, but last Christmas there wasn't much difference in her hair, she can't have had quite a bit taken off. Maybe she just had a trim. I read the last sentence again, *Gabriel wouldn't hear of it.*

He goes straight into the kitchen when he gets home, he seems to be in a good mood. He whistles as he prepares dinner, slicing carrots into thin batons with the sharp kitchen knife, it is so sharp that I daren't use it. I can just imagine slipping and cutting myself deeply and not even noticing it, not feeling it because the cut would be so thin, not realizing until the chopping board was covered in blood. Gabriel is not afraid of knives, he handles this one with confidence, cutting thin pieces of carrot that will soften as soon as they hit the heat, mingling with the slender strips of leek that have already been prepared and are waiting in a bowl, they will look pretty against the blue-and-white china. He is still whistling as he opens a bottle of wine, pours a glass.

"Would you like a drink?"

He holds up the glass, smiling. The light from above shines through the dark wine making it glow red, it's a lovely color.

I nod, he puts the glass in front of me, pours himself one. I sit down at the kitchen table and leaf distractedly through a fashion magazine that came in the mail for Stella, her subscription lasts for several more months, it ought to be canceled. He starts whistling again, opens a can of coconut milk. I take a sip of the wine, turn a few more pages. *Celebrity hair special. You too can look like the stars. Long or short? The shape of your face is key!* Suddenly I get an idea.

"I was thinking of having my hair cut," I say.

"Oh yes?" he says, he sounds a little surprised but doesn't turn around, carries on messing with the can opener, it doesn't seem to be working.

"This would look good on me, don't you think?" I say, holding up the magazine to show him a big picture of a French actress with a wavy pageboy style, cut short at the nape of her neck.

He comes and stands beside me at the table, contemplates the picture.

"It's a bit short, isn't it?" he says.

"Is it?"

"You have such beautiful hair."

He places his hand on my head, slides it over my hair and down to my shoulder.

"I think it would be a shame to cut it so short."

I shake my head.

"I've always had long hair, I'm sick of it."

"I think it would be stupid."

I feel him gathering my hair into a bunch at the back of my neck, winding it around his hand.

"Maybe I don't care what you think," I say quietly.

He is pulling my hair now, forcing my head back until I am looking straight up at the ceiling, just like on the patio last summer, but then it felt completely different, it was what I wanted him to do. He leans over me, gazes at me in silence before suddenly letting go of my hair and going back to his chopping board.

"Do whatever you want," he says.

My scalp hurts. He is stronger than he thinks. Or else he knows exactly how strong he is.

I watch him adding chicken to the wok, followed a little while later by the carrots and leeks, he flips them over quickly and decisively. When he has added the coconut milk and is dropping the empty can in the garbage bag he happens to catch it on the edge of the cupboard door, it falls out of his hand onto the floor.

"Fucking *hell!*" he shouts, with such force that I jump. He holds up his hand to show me, there is blood on the inside of his thumb, slowly trickling down toward his palm.

"What happened?"

I quickly move over to him, tear off a piece of paper towel, take hold of his hand, and gently wipe away the blood. It is a small cut that doesn't look particularly deep, it stops bleeding almost immediately, but he still swears several times, kicks the empty can so that it hits the skirting board next to the spot where Nils has his food, spattering coconut milk across the floor and the wallpaper.

———————

The white cardigan is damp from the mist in the air, it looks like a thin layer of crystals sparkling all over the angora, like a covering of snow. It hardly smells of anything after hanging outside to air all morning, glowing white like a ghost in the gray-brown garden. As soon as it has dried I put it on, carefully fastening the small mother-of-pearl buttons. In front of the mirror I put up my hair, tidily, pushing my stubborn curls into place with clips.

In the kitchen I put on the coffee machine, five cups, strong, otherwise he won't drink it. I can hear him upstairs, the sound of the old office chair rolling across the uneven wooden floor from time to time, something falling off the desk with a thud, a book perhaps, from one of the tall, unsteady piles.

There is no really fresh bread, but when I have warmed some small rye rolls in the oven they smell newly baked. I fill them with ham and paprika, breaking off small sprigs of parsley from the bunch in a glass on the kitchen windowsill, the parsley seems to stay green and fresh all winter, presumably because the weather is so mild, the taste is slightly more bitter than it was in the summer, but it looks pretty on the rolls.

I pour coffee into two of the blue-and-white cups, add milk to mine, place everything on a tray. He usually has something to eat around this time, but sometimes he forgets. Both of us forget mealtimes, it's as if they no longer meet an actual physical need but are simply a ritual, a habit.

There are seventeen steps leading to the upper floor, I have counted them. Soon I will know this house inside out.

He is sitting at his desk with his back to the door, but spins around on the old office chair as soon as he hears me. He stiffens when he catches sight of me, he looks amazed for a brief moment, then his expression darkens.

"What the hell are you doing?" he says.

I don't know how to respond. I don't even know what he means until I see him staring at the cardigan, at the row of gleaming buttons.

"I don't know, I thought . . ." I begin. "You did tell me to wear it."

"I certainly did not."

I put the tray down on the bureau.

"I've made something to eat if you're hungry," I say quietly.

"Take the cardigan off."

His tone is sharp, and when he gets to his feet I recoil, he takes a step toward me.

"I thought you'd like it."

It is impossible to read anything from his expression, for a second I almost think a smile flits across his face, a kind smile, as if he were doing this for my own good, or at least believed that was the reason. I don't like not knowing, I don't like it when something in his eyes is incomprehensible, incalculable. This isn't normal, I think, but then nothing here is normal, I back away slowly. When he quickly moves toward me I turn around and run, through the bedroom and down the stairs, seventeen steps, my feet clattering down each one, I grab hold of the worn, shiny banister so that I won't fall on the curve of the staircase, I run through the hallway and into the guest bedroom. I can hear his footsteps on the stairs, he is right behind me. I slam the door shut, place my hand for the first time on the big black wrought iron key in the lock. When I turn it to the right the barrel follows without any problem, sliding into place with a heavy click. I think about Stella's words that first evening, *Nothing works properly around here*, perhaps she was talking about more than just the awkward window catch. I try the door, it's locked. My heart is pounding.

The next moment the handle is pushed down from the outside, without success. He mutters something.

"Marina?" he says in a loud voice. "What are you doing?"

He pushes the handle down again, tugging at it to check that he really can't get in.

I move backwards, sit down on the bed, on the crocheted bedspread, looking at the door, at the handle, which he pushes down experimentally several more times.

"Marina?"

His voice is gentler now. I unbutton the cardigan, pull it off, and throw it in a heap on the floor. Then I notice that I am crying, I wipe the wetness from beneath my eyes, looking at the door. It's cold without a cardigan, it's cold everywhere downstairs apart from the kitchen and living room. I gather up the crocheted bedspread, place it around my shoulders, curl up underneath it. I hear him talking on the other side of the door.

"You scared me," he says. "You understand that, don't you? You're so alike sometimes, you and Stella. Open the door now. I didn't mean to get angry, I'm sorry."

He knocks tentatively.

"Marina? Open the door."

After a while he gives up, I hear his footsteps in the hallway, running water in the kitchen, the clatter of dishes in the sink. I curl up under the bedspread and fall asleep.

It is already dark outside when I wake up, I can see only my reflection in the windowpane. It is still afternoon but the house is silent, it could just as easily be the middle of the night. I turn the key cautiously and open the door of the guest room, just a little crack. The hallway outside is dark and empty, I can see a light from the kitchen, a triangle of light falling on the rag rug on the hall floor. I can hear the faint sound of music, I don't recognize it.

He is sitting in the living room, reading. There is an LP on the stereo, a fire is burning in the tiled stove. He smiles when he sees me in the doorway, closes his book.

"Darling."

He's never called me that before. Nobody has called me that before. You don't say that unless you mean it, I think, that's what he said to Stella last summer, the same tone, his voice can sound so soft. I still have the bedspread around my shoulders, I feel slightly dizzy, that's what happens when you fall asleep in the middle of the day, it feels as if it ought to be morning. I meet his gaze.

"Did you fall asleep?" he says in the same kindly tone of voice. "Come and sit with me for a little while."

He pats the sofa encouragingly, the way you entice a pet, he is still smiling when I sit down beside him. Then he kisses me, places his hand on the nape of my neck, draws me to him, runs his finger down my cheek.

"You've got a pattern on your face," he says with a smile and I feel at my cheek, the bedspread has left an impression.

He puts his arm around my shoulders and picks up his book again, opens it and begins to read, he seems absorbed in it straightaway.

Were things like this between the two of them, I wonder? Quarrels and reconciliation, over and over again, always because he got angry about something, lost control, frightened her. It's strange that she didn't write more about it in her diary, I think, in its pages her life comes across as balanced, almost boring. I remember the entry about getting her hair cut, the laconic *Gabriel wouldn't hear of it.* And suddenly I understand: she knew he would read her diary. He must have known it was there in the drawer of the bedside table, it's unthinkable that he wouldn't have opened it and read it. Perhaps more for his own sake than out of any concern over how she was feeling, more a kind of self-obsessed curiosity about whether she had written anything about him. And she understood that, of course. That's why her entries were so short, so impersonal. That's why she wrote *Gabriel wouldn't hear of it* about something that frightened her so much she ran weeping all the way across the field to Anders and Karin. Because she knew that was the way he would want to remember it.

His arm around my shoulders feels heavy now, I shrug it off, get up from the sofa, he looks at me in surprise.

"I'll go and let Nils in," I say.

"He's already in."

"I'll go and get something to read."

His eyes follow me as I leave the room.

"There's tea if you'd like some," he shouts when I am already in the kitchen, I don't answer him.

I can barely hide my relief when he says he's going to drive into town the following morning. He has hardly pulled onto the little gravel road in front of the house before I am upstairs. I have already gone through all the closets and cupboards in the bedroom, all the piles of newspapers, magazines, and catalogs, all the books on the shelves, there was nothing there. I walk round and round the bedroom not knowing where to search, I sit down on the bed, open the drawer of the bedside table and look at the pale-blue notebook, feel at the base of the drawer. It could be a false bottom, I think, there could be a space underneath it where you can hide things, but there isn't, it's just a thin sheet of wood, I knock on it several times to prove it to myself, push the drawer shut.

I kneel down next to the bed, start feeling at the back of the bedside table, under the shelf that used to house books and magazines, there is nothing there. I glance under the bed, it's an empty space, I feel inside the frame of the bed and there, right up at the top, my fingertips touch something. I immediately recognize the cool, shiny silk, I lie down on the floor and peer under the bed. Attached to the inside of the frame is a similar notebook to the one in the drawer, but this one is dark red, I try to pull it free, get a firm grip on it, it comes away with a tearing sound. There are two wide strips of Velcro on the back, and on the inside of the bed frame.

I realize my hands are shaking as I open the book, it is by no means full, but the pages are covered in Stella's neat handwriting, short entries, all undated.

Perhaps it IS stupid just like everyone thinks, even if no one actually says it, I don't know. In some way it feels as if I've made my bed and now I have to lie in it—I don't really like it when people portray themselves as some kind of martyr, I've seen it so many times, the way they seem to derive strength from a role that is in fact purely destructive. I don't know what you ought to demand or what you ought to settle for, that's a terrible phrase, "settle for," but I suppose that's the way it is for a lot of people, I've often had that feeling about couples I've met in town, in the stores, at parties; they don't even seem particularly fond of one another, it's more as if they're simply used to one another, I used to think it was terrible but now I don't know anymore. I have no intention of being a martyr, I have no intention of feeling like one, not even when things seem difficult; he's just as much of a martyr as I am in those situations, he knows as well as I do that this isn't perfect, but this is the way it's turned out, perhaps there is some merit in making the best of the situation.

I am sometimes afraid of him when he's angry. Sometimes it feels as if I'm provoking it although I

*don't do anything specific, it's as if my presence is all
it takes. I've given a lot of thought to what kind of
father he would be, although I'm sure there wouldn't
be any difference, he would carry on being just
the way he is now: someone you try not to annoy,
someone you try to keep in a good mood.*

*We have nothing in common whatsoever. Sometimes
he isn't even particularly pleasant, not even in the
company of others, it annoys me and it embarrasses
me. And yet no one ever asks what I see in him
because he's so good-looking, and that's why no one
wonders. If he wasn't, they would ask.*

*He was too rough with me again yesterday. It's not just
in the bedroom now, he doesn't seem to be aware of what
he's doing: I wanted to get up from the sofa, he wanted
me to stay, it was playful at first, I think. I've got a bruise
on my arm now, it doesn't show if I wear long sleeves.*

*I have thought so many times that I ought to move
away from here.*

*Everything he does, I think he believes it's for my
sake, in some way.*

*My period is late. I don't know whether to tell him or
not.*

*I miss M, there has been some kind of barrier
between us, I don't know if that's normal between
sisters, but now I think the relationship between
siblings can take many different forms, just like other
relationships: I am so much older than her, so it's
hardly surprising that we have never been as close as
some other sisters. I enjoyed having her here, I would
like us to see each other more often from now on. I
said that to her before she left, she seemed pleased.*

Stella did indeed say that, on the platform just as I was about to get on the train, the tears spring to my eyes as I remember. That was the last thing we said to each other, promising that we would try to meet up more often in the future.

*It didn't work this time either. I don't know how I'm
going to tell G.*

It didn't work, at first I don't understand what she means, then I realize it's exactly as I thought, ever since last summer in fact, even if I have never dared to think it through to its conclusion. Now I recall exactly how she wept in my arms on the park bench in the palace garden last summer, *He got so angry. Furious, almost.* That is the last entry in the book.

My heart is pounding now. *Where shall we go then*

for pastime, if the worst that can be has been done, we have to be together. His grip on my wrists, I want it, in a different way from her. She says it herself, after all, I think, it's as if her presence is all it takes to annoy him, more than mine, I can learn what to do, there's nothing odd about that, you just avoid irritating him, avoid provoking him. The pictures are flickering through my mind now, when I see Stella down at the lake she is not alone, she is not trying to hold her breath underwater and misjudging the situation, she does not slip and bang her head on a rock, he is there with her, he is the one holding her head down, staring at her under the water, watching her hair billowing slowly beneath the surface, her dress opening out like a flower around her body, like a water lily, a lily, wasn't that what he said. *I am sometimes afraid of him when he's angry,* I won't make him angry.

He suddenly shouts from downstairs that dinner is ready, I hadn't even noticed he was home. He sounds pleasant, normal, I don't know what to do with the diary, I am still holding it in my hand as I walk down the stairs, I have to ask him, I have to say something, he has to explain and I have to explain and then we can move on. I understand, I will say, I understand that you got angry with her, and not just angry, you were disappointed, upset, I understand that. Tell me what happened, I will say in my nicest voice, he likes telling me things. He likes the fact that I am a good listener. I put the diary down on the bureau in the hallway, sit down at what has become my place at the dining table, he smiles at me.

We eat in silence. I am afraid of saying things in the wrong way, I repeat sentences in my head, I will say that secrets bind people together. I will say that I understand. He has made a pasta gratin, ham, Feta cheese, a salad, simple everyday food, but delicious, everything he makes is delicious. We drink wine, the kitchen clock on the wall ticks loudly, I have never thought about it before, never noticed how loud it is, it bothers me.

"Is that clock new?" I have to ask even though I know it's a completely unfeasible idea.

"No."

"I just didn't recognize it, that's all. Or rather, I didn't recognize the sound."

I spear a piece of tomato with my fork, chew it for so long that it has completely dissolved in my mouth before I swallow it. If we are going to be together he has to know that I know, I think. That I believe things will be different now, that I am convinced things will be different. That I am better for him than Stella. I have known it all along, I have known it ever since she told me about him for the very first time, he has known it too, I think, perhaps he realized it straightaway, that first evening last summer, there was something about his expression when we first said hello, he held my gaze, held on to my hand.

"I've read Stella's diary," I say.

He raises his eyebrows, looks at me.

"Oh?"

"It says you hurt her."

He shakes his head.

"No, it doesn't."

"Not in the diary you read. She had another one."

He looks surprised for a moment, but seems to recover himself quickly.

"So what did she write in the other one?" he says.

"Everything. Everything she didn't write in the one she knew you used to read. How she really felt. The fact that she was afraid of you sometimes when you got angry, and how angry you were about her miscarriages. And that you hurt her."

"I did nothing to her that she didn't want me to do. You understand that, surely?"

"It says you did."

I realize as I am speaking that I am not saying what I had intended to say at all, but he is not reacting as I expected him to react either, he is so defensive.

"I might have been a little careless on the odd occasion, given her the odd bruise by mistake . . . but never more than that," he says. "If she wrote anything different, then I'm sure it was just fantasies. She had quite a lot of fantasies like that."

I shake my head.

"No, obviously you don't want to believe that."

He gives me a wry smile.

"But the two of you are more similar than you think. She liked it, just as you like it. Although you do seem to like it more."

"She was intending to leave you," I say. "If she hadn't gotten pregnant, she would have left you."

"Is that what she wrote?"

"Yes."

He has gotten up from the table, his glass clinks on the draining board as he puts it down. The clock on the wall is ticking loudly now, I think it sounds irregular, some seconds are far too long, as if the hand is hesitating before marking each second, unsure whether it wants to continue into the future or not.

"She would never have done that. She knew she was mine."

I am still looking down at the table, my fingertips tracing the lines of the ornate pattern on the cloth. There must be something wrong with the clock. Gabriel ought to change the battery.

"Do you hear me?"

He sounds a long way off now. Daffodils, narcissi, tiger lilies in the pattern on the cloth, I touch the anthers of the tiger lilies, thinking of the lilies behind the greenhouse, of that first evening when I arrived here in the summer, how clean the air felt, how vast the sky was in all directions, it was utterly still, a perfect summer's evening. Stella showed me around, the greenhouse, the tiger lilies, the bluebells growing in the remains of the stone wall, she told me not to go too close, she said there were adders among the stones. When we were little we went to visit friends who had rows of tiger lilies in their borders, Stella and I touched the anthers, got rusty brown pollen all over our fingers, it was like pigment, difficult to wash off later, it stained our skin.

I think about his hand around my wrists, the weight of his body on mine, the firmness of his grip. He knows exactly how strong he is. I am suddenly disgusted by myself when I think about how much it aroused me, the feeling of not being able to free myself, of being totally at his mercy.

"What actually happened?" I say, quietly at first, and then I realize this is precisely the question he ought to answer, and I say it again, "What actually happened?" My voice is more confident now, it's a question I should have asked before, as soon as they found her, or even last summer when I realized things weren't right between Stella and Gabriel, I can hear Gabriel's voice now, he tries to talk over the top of me but I shake my head, "You were with her, weren't you?" I say, "Did she look like a flower afterwards? Under the water?"

He yells at me, telling me to calm down.

"You're hysterical," he roars. "You're just like your sister."

That shuts me up. I feel the tears spring to my eyes.

"No I'm not," I whisper, I don't know if he hears me. I feel feverish now, exhausted and frozen, the room seems to be spinning around, not just the floor but the walls, the cooker, the window overlooking the garden, the door leading into the living room, the cooker again, the door leading to the hallway, the windows, I can just see the apple tree at Anders and Karin's through the bare fruit trees in the garden, it is misty outside, I can only just see it, the cooker, the door to the hallway again.

"Marina," he says in his soft voice over by the sink, it's as if I am hearing him from a distance. "Stop making a fuss now, darling."

I recognize the look in his eyes, it's the same as it was in the bedroom when he got angry because I was wearing Stella's cardigan, it's a look that seems to be full of anger and concern at the same time. He takes a few steps toward me, and I jump up from the chair and run toward the door, it feels as if the whole room is tilting now, like a ship in choppy waters, I grab hold of the doorpost for support then carry on out through the hallway, through the curtain, the back porch, Stella's boots are standing there, I quickly push my feet into them. My hands are shaking as I clumsily unlock the door, I hurry outside and down the steps, out onto the lawn, I can hear Gabriel on his way out of the house, I hear the rattle of the bamboo curtain, all the little wooden tubes dancing as he pulls it to one side.

"Marina!" he shouts, I keep on going, right to the end of the lawn, I know exactly where I'm going. A small ditch separates the garden from the field next door, I step over it easily, the exterior lights reach this far but after a few steps the darkness wraps itself around me. The field is muddy and wet, my feet slip and slide. It is a mild evening, there is a fine drizzle in the air, almost standing still, the air is milky, thick. I hear Gabriel call my name again, he seems to be in the garden still but I don't turn around, I keep on going, stumbling, it is so dark, the sky high above me, velvet black and studded with stars beyond the mist, like a wet curtain between me and space. I can see the apple tree at the end of the field, the glow of its lights flowing out into the wet air, its outline is blurred but it is clearly visible, like a lighthouse on the horizon. I fix my gaze on it. It's not far, it didn't take me long to walk there when I went up the road and it's a shorter distance across the field, as the crow flies, I remember the first time I heard that expression, Stella explained it to me when I was little, the

shortest distance between two places, the route a
bird would take. I remember picturing it in my head,
the same picture that still comes back to me whenever I hear the expression: a bird plunging down the
steep slope leading to the water at my parents' house,
speeding across the water and the cornfield on the
other side, it is always summer in my mind, the air is
always clear, the corn yellow and ripe, there was no
bridge, you had to go all the way around, it was closer
as the crow flies.

It is quiet, the darkness is immense all around me,
I can hear only the sound of my own breathing, and
my steps in the mud, I haven't the strength to run
anymore. My feet squelch with every step, Stella's
boots are slightly too big I realize now, perhaps half a
size, I used to inherit her boots when we were little,
and her shoes, always half a size too big. We picked
flowers on the morning of midsummer's eve every
year to make into garlands, this is an early memory,
old, I was little, it was me and Stella and Mom, we
wore our best dresses with our Wellington boots because there might be snakes, you never knew if there
might be snakes. That was by a field too, the horizon
far away and there were cornflowers and red clover
and daisies at the edge of the field, our best dresses
and our Wellington boots, a little bit too big, flapping
at my heels, the smell of rubber and freshly ironed

cotton and an early summer's morning. The garlands
soon wilted, the white petals of the daisies, slimy and
drooping, the red clover lasted best, tough stems,
hard to break, Mom taught Stella the names of the
flowers and Stella taught me. *Trifolium pratense*, am
I crying or is it the rain? Every step takes an eternity
now, my whole body is exhausted, I want to lie down
here, simply sink to the ground, my dress is like a wet
membrane around my body, a wet carapace that has
stuck fast to me, like the cocoon butterflies have to
wriggle out of before they can fly away on wings that
are brand-new, delicate, trembling. Stella and I found
a caterpillar in the garden once, fat and furry on a
branch, we put it in a jar, a big jar that had once held
gherkins, several kilos of gherkins that we had eaten
with our Sunday dinner and our bubble-and-squeak,
and we looked up the caterpillar in a book about insects: the tiger moth, it overwinters as a caterpillar
known as a woolly bear, the book said it eats willow,
we searched out a tree in the forest and fed it and it
took big bites of the leaves, we could hear it munch-
ing as it ate, we giggled as we listened to it. Then it
turned into a chrysalis, a white cocoon on one of the
branches, we kept the jar in the garden shed along
with the lawn mower and wood for the stove and
fishing rods and a hammock and a croquet set. This
was in the spring, a chilly March, April maybe, still

frosty at night, the moss on the lawn beneath the lilac bushes was white in the mornings, crunching underfoot when you walked across it, leaving darker footprints where the frost had melted beneath the soles of your shoes. The caterpillar was gone one morning, the jar was empty, Stella said it had turned into a butterfly and flown away and I wondered how it had managed to get out of the jar, the air holes in the lid were so small. It was many years before she told me it had died, that it had turned into a butterfly and died in the jar, wriggled out of its cocoon and been ready to fly away, but it had been unable to get anywhere, perhaps it had died of exhaustion during its attempts to find a way out of the jar, it had been lying motionless on the bottom of the jar one morning, she and Mom had found it before I woke up and agreed not to say anything to me.

The tree is suddenly closer. Am I moving my feet? I have to look down, I can hardly see my boots, I am so tired, I want to lie down now, curl up somewhere warm. Perhaps I would be able to retain my body heat if I were to lie down on the ground right here and curl up, I could wait for morning, wait for someone to find me, wrap me in a blanket, speak to me gently and tell me that everything will be all right.

Suddenly I hear Gabriel's voice, I hear him calling my name across the field, he sounds far away but it's difficult to tell, the dampness in the air muffles every sound, insulates, wraps itself around the sound waves like wadding and cotton wool. Perhaps he is closer than I think, perhaps he is right behind me, following the sound of my footsteps and my breathing, he will soon be right behind me, he will place his hand on my shoulder. He is strong, his firm grip on my wrist, his body on top of mine, heavy, I wouldn't be able to free myself even if I really tried. I peer behind me, trying to see something, a movement, an outline, trying to listen for footsteps. But everything is quiet, empty, my breath turns to vapor as it comes out of my mouth, it is suddenly chilly, the air is clearer and the contours of the apple tree are sharper now, is there snow in the air? The first snow? It is December now, I have lost track of the days, and the weeks in fact, I don't know how long I've actually been here, or how long I've been in this field, ten minutes? An hour? I should be colder, it's strange that I'm not. The new chill in the air sharpens my brain, I take a deep breath, look up, the sky is clear and full of stars now. The North Star shines bright and cold, almost immediately above Anders and Karin's apple tree, around it I can make out constellations I thought I had forgotten, I suddenly remember their names: the Great Bear and the Little Bear, the Big Dipper, Orion's Belt, Cassiopeia, Dad taught me, he had a star chart, we used to stand on the balcony at home looking up, the clear winter evenings were best, the entire sky was a vast sparkling dome above us.

Then there is only one ditch left, the ditch separating Anders and Karin's garden from the field, I am just about to step across it when I stop for just a moment, enchanted. The grass is sparkling beneath the apple tree with all its lights, it is frosty now, frozen mist, the whole garden is covered in a white frosting, it is so beautiful, it looks so peaceful. I breathe out, I see the apple tree glittering through my steaming breath.

Then he grabs hold of my arm. His grip is hard and takes me completely by surprise, I spin around, try to pull away but instead my feet slip. Beneath the thin layer of frost the ground is still soft, perhaps there will be no deep frost this winter. The grass slides against the mud beneath my feet, I slip, fall, he doesn't loosen his grip on my arm but falls with me, he looks surprised as he loses his balance. He lands half on top of me, muttering a curse.

I can feel one elbow aching, I must have banged it when I fell, but nothing else hurts, it's nice to lie down even though it's cold, I am so tired, too tired to be afraid anymore. Perhaps Gabriel can see it in my face, the fact that his quarry has been brought down, that I am not going to offer any further resistance, because he doesn't attempt to hold on to me. Instead he sits up, looks at me.

"What happened?" he says.

I have to close my eyes, I am so tired. I can feel how the frost has melted underneath me, turned to moisture that has been sucked up by my dress, I will leave an impression of my body in this spot, like a gingerbread man cut out of floury dough, I realize I am so cold I am shaking.

"I'm so tired," I say.

———

I don't know how we got home. Perhaps Gabriel dragged me back across the field, perhaps I managed to walk under my own steam. I remember warm water on my body and when I wake up I am wearing my nightdress and panties, I am lying in the big bed upstairs, with an extra blanket on top of the duvet. Gabriel is sitting on the bed looking at me.

"How are you?" he says.

I shrug my shoulders.

"I don't know."

My voice sounds hoarse, my throat is sore. I realize I hurt all over when I try to move, my whole body feels tender, as if every muscle is aching slightly from too much exercise. Twilight is falling, the clock radio by the bed is showing half past two in the afternoon, the sky is unusually clear with just a few fluffy clouds on the horizon, burning pink and yellow. I can tell by the light outside the window that the snow which fell last night is still lying. The room is warm, it smells of hyacinths and cigarette smoke, I understand why when I see the big ashtray with the brass dolphin on the bedside table. One cigarette still glows among the pile of stubs. The daily paper lies next to the ashtray, with one of the blue-and-white coffee cups on top of it. I realize Gabriel has been sitting on the edge of the bed for a long time, waiting for me to wake up.

He looks at me, contemplates me with that dark, serious expression for a few seconds before he leans over and kisses me. I return the kiss, he touches me, his hands pull away the covers and slide down my arms, down my body and my thighs, I close my eyes.

Suddenly I feel a stabbing pain on the inside of my thigh, high up, at first I have difficulty in placing the sensation and my initial thought is that something is biting me, a snake, that something has penetrated my skin and is on its way into my bloodstream, some kind of poison, a fever, I can almost feel it spreading through my body, I know that when it reaches my heart I will die. Then the stabbing turns into a different type of pain, deeper, it feels strange, ice cold or red hot, at first I can't decide which. Then it hurts so much I have to scream, and he leans over me and kisses me again, holds me tight and presses his lips to mine, suffocating my scream, it is such a passionate kiss that for a moment I forget the pain and then it is gone and only the kiss remains and I am kissing him back, clinging to him, he gently caresses my thigh, brushes against the mark, I feel another stab of pain.

He gets up and stubs out the glowing cigarette in the ashtray, gazes at me as I lie there with my thighs parted, his expression is dark and warm at the same time, he lies down beside me again, buries his face in my hair and whispers in my ear that I have been a good girl.

When he has fallen asleep I gently extricate myself from his arms and slide out of bed. My body feels stiff, the floor is cold to my bare feet, I push them into a pair of slippers that happen to be in the bedroom. Even though it is dark in the room the mark on my thigh is clearly visible in the mirror, burning dark against my winter-pale skin, I touch it cautiously with my fingertips. In spite of the fact that it hurts it is not unpleasant, it is something else. This is the proof, I think.

I make my way carefully down the stairs, I have begun to learn how to avoid the spots that creak the most. The scent of hyacinths fills the entire house, soft and perfumed. It is as if the change in the weather has affected the whole atmosphere, even indoors, as if the house itself has relaxed beneath its blanket of snow, grown calm and still.

There isn't a sound downstairs. I cross the hallway and the porch to let Nils in, he meows and slides in through the door as soon as I open it, padding quickly toward his food dishes in the kitchen. The air outside is fresh, chilly. I inhale deeply, drawing it into my lungs, it feels as if my brain immediately becomes clearer.

When I have closed the outside door I notice the pot on the bureau. It must have been there ever since that Friday evening, I have lost track of the days. It is cold in the porch, there is no heating, and dark, only a small amount of light seeps in through the old beveled glass in the window of the outside door. Too dark for an orchid, I think, perhaps just as dark as down on the floor of the rain forest. And nothing to climb up in order to get closer to the light.

The whole plant is slimy and drooping, collapsed. The pink flower is dark, the stem soft and rubbery. I take it through to the kitchen, open the cupboard under the sink, and drop the pot in the garbage bag.

The darkness outside the window is different now, less dense. The field that extends on the far side of the garden is covered in snow, a thin layer, it gleams in the darkness. Stella's diary with the shiny red cover, what happened to that yesterday? I had it in my hand when I ran through the house last night, but what happened to it after that?

Perhaps I dropped it in the field, somewhere on the way toward Anders and Karin's apple tree. In my mind's eye I can see it lying there, in the mud that is frozen now, it is covered with snow, the words inside it will be dissolved by the dampness, they will be obliterated, disappear. I can see it lying there as the snow melts and the muddy earth becomes soft and wet, until the time for the spring sowing arrives, the farmer who cultivates the land will plow the field and the sharp blades of the plow will slice through it, shredding it into strips of white and red, digging them down into the ground. And then he will scatter seed across the field, seed that will germinate and sprout, growing into corn that will stand ripe and yellow beneath next summer's sun.